Eloise

Eloise

A Love Story

Alina Gomes

ARCHWAY PUBLISHING

Archway Publishing books may be ordered through booksellers or by contacting:

Archway Publishing
1663 Liberty Drive
Bloomington, IN 47403
www.archwaypublishing.com
1 (888) 242-5904

Because of the dynamic nature of the Internet, any web addresses or links contained in this book may have changed since publication and may no longer be valid. The views expressed in this work are solely those of the author and do not necessarily reflect the views of the publisher, and the publisher hereby disclaims any responsibility for them.

Any people depicted in stock imagery provided by Thinkstock are models, and such images are being used for illustrative purposes only. Certain stock imagery © Thinkstock.

ISBN: 978-1-4808-4001-0 (sc)
ISBN: 978-1-4808-4000-3 (hc)
ISBN: 978-1-4808-4002-7 (e)

Library of Congress Control Number: 2016920603

Print information available on the last page.

Archway Publishing rev. date: 12/28/2016

To my precious daughter and grandchildren
who are the true loves of my life.

CONTENTS

May the road rise to meet you.
May the wind be ever at your back.
May the sun shine warm upon your shoulder
and the rains fall soft upon your fields.
And until we meet again, may God
hold you in the palm of his hands.

—Irish blessing

CHAPTER ONE

Eloise's first few weeks in this world were a struggle. She was born premature, and the doctors thought she wouldn't make it. They didn't give her parents much hope. God had other plans for Eloise, though. She survived, and, although she was a small child, she was healthy.

Eloise lived with her family in Brazil and had three sisters and two brothers. When she got to be four years old, Eloise still didn't have much hair—only fine blond wisps. "Mommy," she said, "I want to have beautiful hair."

"Don't worry, Eloise," her mother said. "Someday you will have long, thick, beautiful hair."

As Eloise got older, she did become very beautiful. She was still delicate and, at five feet two inches, quite petite. Years of ballet dancing had given her a sculpted, perfectly proportioned body. She was also gifted with flawless skin and long, thick hair. She was the envy of many girls.

Eloise was not only beautiful but also very perceptive and intelligent. She got good grades all through school. She studied ballet and loved to perform. She dreamed of becoming a professional ballet dancer and an actress. Her parents were strict, though, and they didn't approve of their precious youngest daughter entering show business. In their minds, the best profession for a young lady was that of schoolteacher—but only for a little while. Ultimately, they expected Eloise to get married and have a family.

As for boyfriends, dating wasn't easy. Eloise's parents had a strict curfew, and most of her time was consumed by her studies. She did flirt here and there, though, and when she was sixteen, she had her first kiss. She was terrified her parents would find out that a boy had kissed her. He moved away before things could get serious. Eloise didn't worry. She knew that one day she would meet a special man and fall in love.

Eloise mostly kept her hopes and dreams to herself. With five siblings, she relished her privacy. There was one person she confided in—her godmother. Eloise could always count on her godmother for support.

When it came time for Eloise to go to college, her godmother advised her to study foreign languages so that she could become a linguist. Eloise was skilled in learning languages and was fascinated by the complexities of language. She excelled in her studies, but ballet continued to be her passion.

One day, Eloise's father announced that he had decided to move the family to a bigger city where his children would have more opportunities and could attend better colleges. Eloise was ecstatic. Moving to a bigger city would also give her the opportunity to pursue ballet and acting. She could even start taking acting lessons. Maybe she would become a professional ballerina and an actress, after all.

Eloise began to attend a renowned acting school where many respected actors had gone. The main instructor was a world-famous Italian actor and director. Vittorio De Sica had been his mentor.

One day, the instructor called Eloise into his office. "Eloise," he said, "I've seen your progress over the past few months, and I'm impressed. You have a way of really becoming one with a character. You transform yourself. It's a rare skill and one that can't be taught."

"Thank you, sir," Eloise said. She felt her cheeks turn pink as she received his praise. "It is my dream to be a great actress."

"Well, I think you have a good shot, Eloise," he said. "Just stay true to your dream and let me know if there is any way I can help."

Eloise was so grateful for the support from her acting teacher. He introduced her to directors and sent her on theater auditions. It seemed like Eloise's career was about to take off. But then her parents intervened. They wouldn't allow her to play any role that involved kissing on stage. Instead, they insisted she only act in plays for children.

Her parents' rule drastically limited Eloise's options as an actress. She decided to put her theater career on the back burner. She focused on college, taking extra classes and summer courses. By age twenty, she had earned enough credits to graduate early. Now she had a boyfriend, too. She liked him a lot, but he was possessive.

Eloise accepted that her parents were overbearing, but it didn't go beyond that. She was an independent woman, and she wouldn't put up with a boyfriend trying to run her life. They broke it off after a few months.

Then Eloise met Roger. He was a tall, handsome corporate attorney who was twelve years her senior. Eloise was instantly swept off her feet. Roger's age was part of the attraction. She loved his sophisticated, debonair qualities and appreciated all that Roger had to teach her.

Roger loved Eloise's innocence and sweetness. She was more caring and trusting than any woman he had ever known.

There was one problem. Roger had a wife. They had been separated for a few years and were both going in different directions in their lives. Eloise's parents, however, were not happy. For them, it was bad enough that Roger was so much older. The fact that he was married made the relationship impossible. According to the Catholic Church in Brazil, a divorced person was not allowed to remarry. Roger and Eloise would have to leave the country if they wanted to marry.

Given the circumstances, Eloise's siblings, friends, and even her godmother warned her against seeing Roger. Everyone was certain that Eloise would end up alone and unhappy. Eloise ignored their advice. She loved

Roger, and she was willing to leave the country if that's what she had to do to be with him.

Roger and Eloise became close quickly. Until he met Eloise, Roger had never experienced true love. His wife was an upper-class snob, and his marriage had been a failure from day one. He had stayed with her only because he was a gentleman. She was power hungry and domineering—even in the bedroom, which made lovemaking a disaster.

One day, Roger found his wife with another man. The other man was one of many, but Roger was humiliated because this man was his best friend. His wife told him that she wanted a divorce the same day she told him she was pregnant with his friend's child. After such a betrayal, it was a long time before Roger was ready to date again.

Roger never pushed Eloise into an intimate relationship, although he wanted to be intimate with her. He didn't doubt her affection for him; it was all in the way she embraced and caressed him, but he knew he had to let her make the first move.

They had been together a year when Eloise found out about a scholarship program for graduate school in the United States. There was fierce competition for the scholarship, and she would have to study hard and pass a number of tests, but Eloise had a good chance of getting the scholarship.

When Eloise told Roger about the opportunity, he said, "I'll come with you to the US, and while we are there, we can get married."

"That would be the icing on the cake," Eloise said. If they married in the United States, their union would also be legal in Brazil.

Roger filed for divorce. He and his former wife had no children, and she was in another relationship, so getting a divorce wouldn't be an issue.

Eloise's parents were devastated when she told them she was going to marry Roger. Her mother burst into tears and didn't stop crying. The only solution Eloise could think of was to have Roger come meet her parents. If they met him and saw what a good man he was, maybe they would be happy for her.

Roger visited Eloise's parents' house. They all sat down in the living room together. "I know you must be wonderful parents," Roger said, "because your daughter is the kindest and most loving person I have ever met."

"Thank you," Eloise's father said. "We have always tried to protect Eloise."

"I know that," Roger said. "I love Eloise very much, and I also wish to cherish and protect her. I ask that you please allow me to marry your daughter."

"Eloise," her father asked, "is this what you really want—to leave Brazil and marry Roger?"

"Yes, Father," Eloise said. "I love Roger dearly, and I want to marry him."

"In that case," Eloise's father said, "I accept your decision to marry."

Eloise's mother wiped her eyes. "Then it's decided," she said. "No more tears or arguments. You will be Roger's wife."

"Thank you, Mom. Thank you, Dad," Eloise said, embracing them. "I love you both, and I have great respect for you. Thank you."

Eloise's parents hugged Roger, too. Her mother began crying again, but this time they were tears of joy.

After meeting with her parents, Roger and Eloise took a long walk through the city streets. "Roger," Eloise said, "I love you now more than ever. I know you will take care of me, and I can't wait to become your wife."

"My princess," Roger said, "I love you."

When they were alone together, Roger always called Eloise by pet names like *princess*, *sweet child*, and *light of my life*.

"Roger, darling," Eloise said, "I want to go away with you somewhere private for a week—somewhere we can be alone and away from friends and family."

Roger was surprised. He knew what Eloise was telling him. He agreed to find a beautiful hideaway.

CHAPTER TWO

Roger took time off from work so that he and Eloise could visit a small island paradise. He was a senior member at a corporate firm where there was one other attorney. He and the other attorney had been twenty-six years old when they partnered together and opened the first office in the nation's capital. Now there were offices in all the major cities of Brazil.

Roger flew himself and Eloise to the island on his private jet. Roger was an accomplished pilot. He'd been a major in the air force for six years before retiring to follow his career dreams as a civilian. Roger had wanted to work with his father. He went to law school, becoming a corporate lawyer. But he loved to fly. He owned a small, modern airplane that had all the technology it needed. It carried six people. Most of the time, he flew with a copilot, unless it was a two- or three-day business trip.

When they arrived on the island, Roger showed Eloise to the mansion he had rented for their luxurious vacation. Servants and a personal chef would attend to their every need. As they drove up to the mansion, Roger was pleased to see that it took Eloise's breath away. The immense mansion looked like it was fit for a princess, with huge white columns and a marble entranceway. It was steps from the beach, where the turquoise water seemed to merge with the clear blue sky. The beach was covered in soft white sand. "This is more than I ever could have dreamed of," Eloise said.

On their first night there, they walked out onto the terrace after dinner, carrying their glasses of champagne. There was a soft hammock set up out there, and Eloise and Roger curled up together on it.

"Eloise," Roger said, "there is something I have to tell you. It's something I've been meaning to tell you for a long time."

"What is it, Roger?" Eloise asked. Roger took a deep breath. Eloise could see from the worried creases around his eyes that he was afraid to say what he was about to say. He took her delicate hands in his.

"I love you very much, Eloise," he said, "but I understand if you don't want to see me again after you hear what I am about to tell you." Tears came into Eloise's eyes. She couldn't imagine life without Roger. What secret could possibly be so terrible that she wouldn't want to see him again?

"This fact has haunted me for a long time," he said. "Eloise, my darling, I am sterile. I can never give you a child."

"Oh, Roger," Eloise said. "What happened?"

"I had mumps when I was a teenager," he said. "The disease affected my sperm. I've tried everything, but the doctors say there is no cure. If you still want to marry me, I am willing to adopt a child or you can try artificial insemination."

Eloise was relieved; she thought Roger was going to tell her something much worse. She grabbed him in her arms. "You fool!" she said. "Do you think I care? I love you." Roger hugged her back and then kissed her. He was so grateful that she understood. "As for artificial insemination," Eloise said, "no thank you. We can think about adopting. Let's talk about it more and see what we decide. You have to remember, Roger, I am one of six children. I always wanted some time and space for myself."

"Eloise," Roger said, "I love you so much."

"You're the love of my life, Roger," Eloise said, "and all I want is to be with you." They kissed again, this time more passionately. Then Eloise pulled away for a moment. "There is something I have to tell you too," she said. Roger nodded to show he was listening. She came closer and whispered in his ear, "I'm a virgin. You are going to be my first."

Roger smiled. "My princess, I suspected that for some time. I thought it was important that you make the first move. That's why you asked me to bring you here, isn't it?"

"Yes," Eloise said. They embraced again. Roger kissed her softly. Then he stood up and led her to the bedroom. At six feet tall, Roger knew he had to be gentle with his tiny Eloise. He wanted her to be completely comfortable. He sat down on the bed, and Eloise stood in front of him. He caressed her face and neck, slowly making his way down to the V-neck of her dress. He could hear her breaths deepen and felt her heartbeat racing. He slowly undressed her, pausing after each item of clothing to kiss another part of her body. After every touch and every kiss, Roger would wait for a moment. This teasing increased Eloise's desire. He could feel her hands gripping his strong shoulders as she whispered, "More, more," begging him not to stop. Finally, when she couldn't wait any longer, Roger penetrated her. The look in her eyes told him that she felt only pleasure, and at the same moment, they reached climax. Eloise screamed out in ecstasy.

They stayed wrapped around each other, still feeling the exhilaration of the orgasm and not wanting the moment to ever end. Then Roger kissed Eloise's face and hands. He put his arms around her, and they fell asleep for the night.

At dawn, Eloise awoke to the warmth of Roger's body next to hers. He was sound asleep. Eloise said a silent prayer, thanking God for the magical night. Then she fell back to sleep. When she woke up again, Roger wasn't there. She looked around the large, beautiful bedroom. It was quiet and peaceful. She thought some more about last night. She never expected to orgasm her first time. She was so happy that she had waited to lose her virginity until she found Roger. He was a mature man who understood how to treat a woman. Just then Roger came in, wrapped in a bathrobe, freshly showered, with his hair still wet. "Good morning, my princess," he said. "Your wish is my command. What would you like for breakfast this morning? I'm famished."

"Me too," Eloise said. "Can we have breakfast on the sunny terrace overlooking the ocean?"

"Of course," Roger said. He picked up the phone and rang for the personal chef, who immediately set about preparing their breakfast. "What do you want to do today?" Roger asked. "We can play tennis or go to the pool or the beach. Anything you want."

Eloise got out of bed and gave Roger a hug and a kiss. "How about a long walk on the beach?" she said. After breakfast, they strolled along the beach, wading in the water and admiring the incredible view. Then they stretched out on the sand and soaked up the sun for a while.

As the week went on, Roger started teaching Eloise how to play tennis—his favorite sport besides golf. They talked nonstop, as if they had just met. Eloise was enchanted by Roger, and sleeping together had tightened their bond. Roger continued to take it slowly with Eloise. He desired her a great deal, but he wanted her to enjoy every minute. One night he whispered to her, "I don't want you to get tired of me."

After a week in paradise, it was time to go home, but the vacation had brought their relationship to a new level. And they had many more vacations to look forward to in the future. Roger promised that someday he would fulfill her dream of visiting Paris.

CHAPTER THREE

Eloise continued to practice ballet, spend time with her family, and study for her scholarship. She had at least another year of studies to complete before she could qualify for the scholarship. She pushed on, working part-time as a paralegal and studying for hours every day.

With their busy schedules, Eloise and Roger had little time together, but that didn't discourage them. Roger often had to go out of town on business trips. Eloise always prayed whenever Roger had to fly his private jet. Oftentimes he would fly alone. Eloise asked Roger to bring a copilot or fly with a commercial airline, but his business was such that he had to go alone sometimes. Whenever she could, Eloise would go along with him, but her busy schedule didn't always allow it, and she hated flying on small planes. It made her airsick. She could see that Roger was a good pilot, though, and that she should not interfere.

Eloise's godmother was always anxious to hear her stories and find out how everything was going with Roger. Of all her siblings, Eloise was closest with her youngest brother, Luiz Carlos, who was thirteen years younger than her. He was an adorable little boy who followed Eloise everywhere. Eloise called him Lui, and he called Eloise Lolo.

Eloise was also very close to her father, whom she admired for his talent and for his love for his wife and children. Her mother was a very devoted Catholic and always a very kind woman. Eloise's parents and siblings were now pleased that she was dating Roger, who was the most desirable bachelor around. They loved Roger's parents too, whom they had known for years.

Roger's parents were very supportive of their decision to leave the country and get married. They knew that, even thought they would miss Roger and Eloise while they were out of the country, they would eventually get to spend more time with them. Roger's father even had Roger sell some of his business holdings so Roger would have enough liquid assets to carry out his desire to move. Money was not a problem for Roger, as he had vast overseas investments in three countries. He was a lucky and wise investor and had learned from his father.

Eloise's family still didn't want her to move away from home, even though they now loved Roger. They continued to try to persuade Eloise to stay, even though they knew she wouldn't give in. Eloise told her family, "I love all of you with all my heart, but I have to follow my dreams." She had given up a lot because of the family's traditions. Some friends and some family members actually stayed away from her because they didn't agree with her decision to marry a divorced man. This hurt Eloise a great deal.

CHAPTER FOUR

Brazil was under a dictatorship, and although it brought peace to the country, other problems arose for those involved in the revolution. Eloise's father would say, "Brazil is such a great country with such a vast territory. This incredible giant would have to survive. Brazil is a country of the future. One day we Brazilians will have to wake up this giant." Brazil is so fertile and has always been protected from natural disasters. Eloise's father would say, "It is up to the Brazilian people to protect this land and not allow any harm to come to it." He was a visionary of the future growth of Brazil. "Maybe not in my lifetime," he would say, "but I have faith it will be good for the generations ahead. One day my children and my children's children will reap the benefits of this great land."

The country went through some difficult times. The first dictator, Vargas, was a great man who was well loved by all. After his death in 1954, Eloise's father, not a politician, volunteered his time to help elect Governor Juscelino Kubitschek as president. As president, Kubitschek was a visionary who built a new capital city in the middle of the country called Brasilia. Nobody wanted to move there at first, but once built, everyone agreed it was the best idea ever. Today Brasilia is a great, thriving city. The country went through some difficult times during the transition, but today

Brazilians look back with great admiration at the genius of this great man. Against all odds, he is a hero today.

The next president, Goulart, was removed from power and sent out of the country in exile. This revolution lasted for just a few days and was resolved without any bloodshed. The majority of the people didn't even know what was going on until it was all over. When the dust settled, those involved were sent to prison, and others left the country in disgrace.

Eloise and Roger's families were happy that everything ended peacefully. As the Brazilians would say, "Let us just live in peace. We are warriors, fighters. We are lovers. We love our samba and the great food we have in our country. Let the wars end and let us be happy. After all, our country is blessed by God."

Whatever changes might come to Brazil, Roger and Eloise were ready to face them together, because they knew love conquers all. Their love for each other would surpass all else. Romeo and Juliet were their heroes.

Once in a lifetime, you come across magic sent from the Lord. Sometimes it comes in an unrecognizable form. You must take a moment to communicate with God when feeling uncertain and afraid. Take a few moments to meditate. Feel the presence of the Lord guiding you to the right path. There you will find the answer and the courage to move forward. Giving in to fear will only lead you to make the wrong decisions. Anger and revenge are not the answer. Say a prayer, talk to your inner soul, and soon you will see the light.

Eloise and Roger understood this and they filled their minds with positive thoughts. It was impossible for anyone to make them feel anger because love was deep within their souls. They chose their close friends carefully and without prejudice. For those few people they were close to, knowing them was a privilege.

CHAPTER FIVE

Eloise's year of studying had come to an end. It was time to take the exams for the scholarship. If Eloise passed the exams, the organization would determine which university she would go to in the United States. Eloise hoped it would be a school in a warm climate. She hated cold weather.

Roger came back from a job out of state to drive Eloise to all her tests. Eloise began with a writing test, then conversational English, and finally the oral tests. She also provided all the details of her education, references from schoolteachers, and every detail of her personal life and family. She was in strict competition with the other students. At the end of the day, Eloise was exhausted but relieved to be finished with the exams. Now she'd have to await the results.

She was nervous about passing, but her professor assured her that she would do well. Her professor was a mentor and a friend, and he was the one who had told Eloise about the scholarship. He'd been encouraging her all year.

After two weeks, the results came in the mail. Roger was with her when she received the envelope, and they both held their breath as she opened it. Eloise slowly read the results aloud. She'd scored the highest grade in all the most important written and oral tests. She jumped up and down and shouted with joy. Then Roger embraced her. He held her tight in his arms and said, "My beautiful princess, I am so proud of you. My love, let's go way for a few days to celebrate your victory. You deserve a rest after all that studying."

"Oh, Roger," Eloise said, "I love you."

Eloise called her parents and told them the news. Even though they were sad because this meant Eloise would be going to the United States, they were proud of her. They knew she was a hard worker and very intelligent, and she would go far in life. Eloise's mother knew that her daughter would be happy because Roger would be with her. Her parents put Lui on the phone, and he asked her, "Lolo, are you going to Disneyland?"

"No, my darling," Eloise said. "I have to go away to study for a year, but I promise that when I go to Disneyland, I will bring you with me."

Eloise went to see her professor to tell him her scores. "Eloise," he said in his British accent, "I knew you could do it. You were always one of my brightest students. You studied at the English Cultural University for seven long years, and now you have mastered several languages. Your pronunciation is flawless. I know you will do great things in America."

Although Eloise had received her test results, she still had to wait to find out what university she would be attending in the United States. The options were narrowed down to four places, and, unfortunately, none of them were in a state with a warm climate. Roger reassured her that after she had completed her studies, they would move to California or Florida. "It doesn't matter where I go," she said to Roger. "If you are by my side, my love, wherever I am will be heaven for me."

Roger was finalizing his business plans and getting ready for their move. They would be leaving in a month. Eloise would start university at the beginning of September. They set about planning their vacation too. It was winter in Brazil, so Roger suggested they go to the Pocos de Caldas, a beautiful winter resort that they had never been to before. They would take the trip a few weeks before leaving for the United States.

The resort was surrounded by beautiful green mountains, and the hotel had every amenity—several pools and hot tubs, a tennis court, a ballroom, and elegant restaurants.

One night, Roger and Eloise had dinner at a rooftop bistro. Up above them, the stars shone brightly. They had finished their appetizers, and Eloise was enjoying the ambiance.

"My love," Roger said, "can we celebrate this evening with a bottle of champagne?"

Eloise hardly ever drank, but since it was a special occasion, she said, "Yes, my love, let's have champagne to celebrate."

When the bottle came, the waiter popped the cork and poured their glasses. Eloise and Roger toasted, and then Roger reached into his pocket and said, "My princess, I have a surprise for you." He pulled out a small black box and opened the top, presenting Eloise with a sparkling blue diamond ring. It was the most brilliant diamond Eloise had ever seen. Then Roger knelt before her, and these magic words came out: "Eloise, will you marry me and make me the happiest man in the world?"

Tears rolled down Eloise's face, and she opened her mouth to respond, but all that came out was "Oh my God." Then she gathered herself and said, "Roger, my love, I will! I will! I will!" She fell into his arms and began to kiss his face as he tried to slide the ring on her finger. She was still crying, and her tears were wetting Roger's face as she kissed and hugged him.

He stood up and gently picked her up in his arms. Then he finally slid the ring on her finger. It was a perfect fit and looked stunning on her delicate finger. The blue of the diamond dazzled next to her skin. Roger explained to Eloise that he had searched high and low for the diamond. When he finally found a rare blue diamond, he searched for a jeweler who would set it exactly in the design he wanted. The blue diamond was encircled with tiny white diamonds. It was the greatest masterpiece the jeweler had ever made.

When Eloise returned home, the first thing she wanted to do was show her mother her engagement ring. Eloise's mother was a jewelry designer, and she came from a family of jewelers. Her father was a goldsmith, and he owned his own jewelry-making business. Eloise's mother was in love with the ring. Eloise asked her mother to put it in the safe. She was afraid of wearing such a valuable piece of jewelry and attracting thieves. "You should wear it," her mother said, "at least when you are with Roger."

Eloise and Roger knew they would be living in the United States for two years, and in one year they would get married. The whole family would come to the United States for the wedding. There was so much to look forward to and so much happening; rarely a day went by that wasn't filled with preparations.

. . .

Roger was traveling to wrap up his work. He would leave his business in the hands of his father, who he knew would take care of every detail. Both Roger and Eloise were surprised and grateful for all the support they were receiving from their families and friends. Roger's mother was so kind and attentive to Eloise, reassuring her that everything would be perfect as they started their lives together in the United States. She told Eloise how much she would enjoy her new life. She had been to many states in the United States. Eloise asked Roger's mother to visit her family as much as possible. "They are so sad," she said. "And my little brother Lui needs a lot of attention and love. I know how much love you have inside you and what a great mother and friend you have been to Roger. Please be with my mom whenever you can." Roger's mother said that was a promise she'd be sure to keep.

Eloise's godmother was happy for her goddaughter but sad to see her go so far away. Since Eloise's birth, she had been her second mother and best friend. Her godmother never got married, so her family was her world. She gave Eloise a beautiful coat that she had designed and made. It had a fur collar and wristbands. Eloise also put her godmother in charge of designing her wedding dress. Eloise's brothers and sisters were so excited for her. They wanted to go to the United States for the big wedding and then to Disneyland.

Roger had to complete two more business trips to finalize all his deals. Since Eloise was done with schoolwork, she was free to travel with Roger. She decided to accompany him on the longer of the two trips; it was two weeks and a distance away from home, in Porto Alegre. Roger would take time off for them to do some sightseeing along the way. This would be Eloise's first time in the south of Brazil. They flew by commercial airline. Roger took care of his business as quickly as possible, reserving all his evenings for Eloise. She loved the city and areas surrounding Rio Grande do Sul. There was so much history in the city of Pelotas, and they went to see Iguacu Falls and took a quick trip to the Argentina border. The people, fashion, and food fascinated Eloise. Roger had been there many times before, so he was the host and tour guide.

One day they were eating lunch, and Eloise said, "The beef is superb; however, my love, I gained some weight eating this incredible cuisine."

"My sweet princess," Roger said, "I don't see a pound extra. You look lovely, radiant, and relaxed. I think it was a great idea for you to come." There had been so much excitement over the move, they were both overdue for some relaxation.

When they returned home, Eloise found out where she would be attending university—in New Jersey. Now she and Roger were ready to start the final preparations for their trip to the United States—it was just two weeks away. They made their flight and hotel reservations. They would spend three nights enjoying New York City before Eloise started at the university in New Jersey. Roger was due to meet some business associates in New York as well. Eloise had never been to New York City, and Roger made arrangements for them to go to a Broadway show and on sightseeing trips. It was the end of the summer, so the weather would be just perfect there.

Six days before they would be leaving to go to the United States, Roger was getting ready to go on his final business trip. He decided to fly his private jet, since it would only take him three hours to get there. He left on a Monday morning, arriving on time for his business appointment. After the second day of meetings, Roger headed to the airport. He checked the flight path, but the weather was not cooperating. It was raining, and there was a little fog. The weather looked clear along the way, though. Roger took off, and a couple of hours later, he lost touch with air traffic control.

CHAPTER SIX

When Roger's plane fell off the radar, air traffic control searched to locate him. Four hours passed, and he still hadn't made contact with the tower. "He could have made an emergency landing without being able to communicate," one of the officers said to another. The authorities decided to send out a search party. Eight hours passed, and still no communication from Roger. The search continued.

Roger was due to land at 11:00 a.m., and at 6:00 p.m. he was still missing. The families had not been notified. The search party did not give up until 9:00 p.m. when it became too dark to see. The search resumed at 6:00 a.m. the next day. It had now been twenty-four hours, and nobody had heard from Roger. At 10:00 a.m., the search party finally spotted Roger's plane on the ground. As they got closer, it became clear that Roger's plane had crashed.

Sifting through the wreckage, the searchers found Roger's body. He was dead. The body was removed and transported to the morgue for an autopsy.

His family would have to be notified immediately. In situations like this, the news was given in person. A police officer was sent to the house of Mr. and Mrs. Strauss, Roger's parents. This was the most difficult part of the police officer's job. He was told Roger was an only child. When he arrived at the Strauss's house, he was unsure of how to deliver the sad news to them. He rang the bell, and Mr. Strauss came to the door.

Roger's father didn't suspect that anything was wrong. He knew Roger was late coming back from his trip, but that had happened many times before—the only thing that was unusual was that Roger hadn't called. The police officer asked to come inside the house.

He asked about Roger's mother. She was out with Eloise and her mother for a girls' lunch. She was expected to return home in a few hours. The officer had to deliver the message anyway. "I am an officer of the state of Rio de Janeiro," he said. "I was requested to deliver some very sad news. I am sorry to tell you that your son, Roger, was in a plane crash. We searched for him for over twenty-four hours. We found his plane; unfortunately, Roger did not survive the crash." Roger's father collapsed, on the verge of fainting. The police officer caught him and gently held him. He sat Mr. Strauss down on the sofa and called the emergency services for help. The maid and chauffer heard the commotion and came running. Mr. Strauss was in such a state of shock that he needed immediate medical attention.

The family's doctor soon arrived and began to administer first aid. Mr. Strauss was stabilized and put in bed. Doctor Justin Andrew promised the police officer he would stay with his patient until his wife's return. The officer went beyond the call of duty by also promising to stay with Mr. Strauss and wait for Mrs. Strauss to arrive.

It was late afternoon when Roger's mother finally returned home. She came into the house with a big smile. She had a great day with her future daughter-in-law and her mother. She was reminiscing about the delicious lunch, the shopping, all the laughter they shared, and then she saw the doctor. Next she saw the police officer in full uniform. She was immediately overcome by fear and puzzlement.

Dr. Andrew didn't know what to say at first. The officer came to his rescue. He asked Mrs. Strauss to sit down for a moment. She asked where her husband was, and the police officer said, "He will be joining us soon, but first we need to have a word with you." She sat down and was quiet and trembling without knowing why. Her personal maid came in and sat next to her. The officer proceeded in a very formal tone. "Mrs. Strauss, your son, Roger, was in a plane crash early yesterday. The cause is pending investigation. We presume that heavy fog had something to do with it. He didn't want to delay his return home and took off from the airport with caution from the tower. His plane went off the radar two hours after taking off. We searched for over twenty-four hours before locating the plane."

Mrs. Strauss interrupted him. "Where is Roger? We haven't heard from him. Is he okay? Please tell me."

Just then Mr. Strauss came into the room with tears in his eyes. He slowly made his way toward his wife, barely able to walk. He knew he had to be next to his wife as she heard the terrible news. He held her hands and told her, "We lost our son." She fell into her husband's arms in disbelief. She couldn't cry—the tears would not come down.

"No!" she said. "He is not dead. I can feel him next to me. I can hear his voice. He will be home very soon. You will see—all of you will see him here soon." Their housekeeper held up a cup of calming tea, prescribed by the doctor, and urged Mrs. Strauss to drink. She was in a state of shock.

Dr. Andrew called for another doctor to come help him decide if both Mr. and Mrs. Strauss needed to be hospitalized. Then he remembered Eloise. She had to be told the news too. Dr. Andrew asked the other physician, Dr. Mario Alves, to stop by Eloise's home and bring her there with both her parents. This way both families would be together to comfort one another.

Dr. Alves went directly to Eloise's house. He told Eloise and her mother that a very important meeting was taking place at Roger's family's home, and they were asked to please come with him. Eloise's father wasn't home from work yet, but they called him, and he said he would come as soon as he could.

Eloise entered the house holding her mother's hand. Mr. and Mrs. Strauss were lying down side by side in the bedroom. Eloise didn't know what to think of this. She looked at her mother and all the other people in the room and immediately asked, "Where is Roger? I haven't heard from him. Isn't he back yet?" The police officer came to sit next to her and gave her the details of Roger's plane losing contact with air traffic control and crashing, but the final outcome was told by the doctor, who gently explained to Eloise and her mother that Roger did not survive the crash. At first Eloise didn't react. She was sure Roger was alive. She would not accept his death. They had a dream. They had a future together. He would not leave her alone in the world. He would be back soon. She stood up, but she was wobbling. Then she lowered down onto her knees, next to her mother. "Mom," she said, "We have to say a prayer together now. Let's all pray. We have to ask God to send Roger back to us. I don't want to live life without him."

Eloise's father walked into the room at that moment. He knew that something had gone terribly wrong. Roger was not present. A police officer and two of the best doctors in town were all gathered around the Strauss family. Eloise ran to him with tears streaming down her face. "Daddy," she said, "we need to pray. We need Roger to be here with us. Please, Daddy, you are so smart. What can we do? I don't want to live life without my Roger. I need you to tell me this is just a bad nightmare. I will wake up soon, right, Daddy?" The room was full of sadness. The eyes of everyone present were filled with tears. Even the officer, who had to be the bearer of the news, could hardly hold back his tears. Eloise continued, "Daddy, please tell everyone we are going to find Roger and bring him back. You will see. We are going to get married and, and, and ... Please, Daddy, please, tell me that I am going to be with Roger soon. Wherever he is, I am going there to be with him."

Eloise and Mr. Strauss were inconsolable. The only thing the doctors could think to do was sedate them. Eloise's parents wanted to take her home but agreed to let her stay at the Strauss's home that night. The families wanted to be together for the night, and their doctors couldn't agree more.

The family wanted to hear the autopsy result as soon as it was available. It was a horrible accident. A few hours later, Roger's death was announced on the news. The whole country knew Roger. He had donated a lot of time and money to children's charities. He was also known for his incredible good looks—he was so tall, with clear blue eyes and a smile to charm anyone. Roger was a gentleman all the way, a great son, and a good citizen. He was so young, barely thirty-five years old.

Eloise and her parents stayed the whole night at the Strauss home. She slept all night due to the heavy sedation. The doctor was at her side, and Mrs. Strauss checked on her and her husband every hour. Eloise's godmother came in the morning, at the request of Eloise's mother, to give them the love and support that they needed so much now.

When Eloise woke up, at first she seemed calm, but then she realized that she was not at home and started to cry again. She looked around and asked for Roger. Her parents and everyone came over and gave her hugs and spoke loving words, but that didn't stop her from screaming loudly and saying that she wanted to die to be with Roger. She said again and again, "I will not live without my love. I must go to be with him. Mom, Dad, Madrinha, please let me go."

Her godmother came close and held her face. She looked at her and said, "One day you will see Roger again, but your mission in this life is not over yet. We will go to our savior one day, but you, my child, have to wait for that day, as all of us must. Roger accomplished his mission here, so God took him back. He is with God now. You will always remember him. He brought love and happiness to all. You were loved by him. He will be looking out for you whenever he is. He was a kind, wonderful man.

"Always pray for him. Ask our Lord to help you heal from your loss. But remember, those who do not wait for their time to meet our Lord and take the easy way out to end their lives will come back to finish their mission in our world. This is the law of our Lord.

"My beautiful Eloise, you were Roger's little princess—remember how he called you that? Thank God for letting him be part of your life. Eloise, there is a saying—I know this may not be comforting to hear—*only the good die young*. That is because our Lord wants to spare them from earthly suffering, and the Lord wants them to be with him sooner than later. Have faith, my child. You will survive.

"We love you so much, and we will all be here for you, to guide and protect you. You had Roger in your life for more than four glorious years. He will now be the spirit who will look after you and guide you. You are so young. You have a great life ahead of you." Eloise was hopeful that she would survive, but at that moment, she was unable to think of the future.

The Strauss family decided to have Roger's body cremated. Although their religion didn't condone cremation, to hold a funeral or a wake was beyond what they could bear. A memorial ceremony would be held just for the families, their personal doctor, and Mr. Strauss's business associate. Then Mr. and Mrs. Strauss went on a retreat away from friends and other family members. They wanted to share together in their grief. They didn't know what to say to anyone else. All flowers that they received were immediately sent to local hospitals and children's centers.

Eloise also retreated to a private location with her parents, brothers, sisters, and many other members of the family. They stayed out of the public eye for two weeks. The country mourned Roger's death for many days.

The final results of the investigation into the accident determined that it was caused by weather. Roger had gotten lost in the heavy fog. It was a sad, terrible accident. The days and weeks went by, and Eloise's family finally returned.

Eloise was late for her trip to the United States for her scholarship program. She was still not well enough to make any decisions about her future. She had a talk with her parents about canceling her trip and not going at all. Her godmother and godfather came to her rescue. After a few hours of talking and a lot of convincing, they asked her to think carefully about her dream, which started years before she met Roger. She had worked so hard for so many years to achieve her goals.

Eloise knew in her heart that Roger was the noblest, most unselfish person. He would want her to pursue her dream, but how could she face life away from her beloved family without Roger by her side? Eloise's godparents told her that they would travel with her to the United States. They would stay in the United States for a couple of weeks to make sure she was in a good place, and they would meet the family she would be living with.

It was Eloise's decision now. Her parents, although very concerned, liked the idea of her godparents escorting her. Eloise knew Roger would have wanted her to go. She had dreams of Roger whispering to her, "Go, my love, it will be good for you. A change in your life is necessary now." Eloise thought about her decision. She needed to get in touch with the cultural center, and she would have to make a decision in a week's time. She went to speak with her professor at the university in person. He already knew about Roger, and he counseled Eloise carefully. After an hour of conversation with her professor and mentor, she said, "I will go. I need to go. I will be all right. There is a lot I want to do, and I won this scholarship after devoting a year to it. I must go. I know that now. Thank you for your support, Professor. I will not disappoint those who believed in me. My parents are on my side, whichever decision I make. For them, for Roger's parents, for the rest of my family, I will go. God will help me to accept Roger's passing. I will be back in two years, and I will make you and everyone proud of me."

CHAPTER SEVEN

Eloise and her godparents immediately began to prepare for their trip. The host family whom Eloise would be living with was ecstatic to hear she was coming. The couple were both professors, and they had three children who could hardly wait for Eloise's arrival. The family had heard about Eloise's tragedy and would take extra care to give her love and support.

Two days before the trip, Eloise could not stop crying. She was so filled with emotion—because of Roger's death and because she was now leaving her family for the first time. She had tried to be strong and not cry, but now she couldn't hold it back. The days were passing quickly. Eloise had made the decision to go to the United States, and now she had to go through with it.

Her little brother Lui was so sad. He went to her room and knocked on the door, saying, "Lolo, why are you crying? Lolo, I will play with you. Don't cry." Eloise realized that her sweet little brother was suffering because she was inconsolable.

She opened the bedroom door, took him by the hand, and said, "Okay, Lui, let's go for a walk. I promise I will not cry anymore, my darling. We will have fun together."

Mrs. Strauss called Eloise and asked her to come for dinner with her parents before leaving for her trip. When Eloise and her parents arrived at the Strauss's home for dinner, they were pleased to see them and were relived that the Strausses were finally taking care of themselves again and looking well. The Strausses promised Eloise that one day they would visit her in the United States.

After dinner, they asked Eloise and her parents to come with them to the library, as they had very important information to share with them. Eloise and her parents followed the Strausses to the library. Mr. Strauss sat down at a large oak desk and pulled a folder out of the top drawer. "Eloise," Mr. Strauss said, "Roger left a will, and in his will he left his estate to you. Roger knew that my wife and I are very wealthy and didn't need his money. He felt that his estate should go to the woman he loved." Eloise was speechless. She looked at her parents—their eyes were wide with shock. None of them had been expecting this, although, knowing Roger, Eloise shouldn't have been surprised. He was generous beyond words.

"Oh, I couldn't take it," Eloise said.

"Please," Mr. Strauss said. "You must accept; this is what Roger wanted. You can donate the money or use it as you please. It's yours."

"If those were Roger's wishes," Eloise said, "then I will take it. I'll ask my uncle, who is my godfather, to handle everything. He's an attorney."

When the day came for Eloise to leave for the United States, all her family, including the Strausses, went with her to the airport to say goodbye. Eloise and her godparents arrived in New York on a beautiful sunny morning. It was the end of August, and the weather was hot and a little humid. They were booked in a hotel by Central Park. On their first night, there they went to see a Broadway show—just as Roger had planned. The next day, they took a walk down Fifth Avenue to see the beautiful shops before taking Eloise to the town where she would attend university.

Eloise's godparents dropped her off at her host family's home in New Jersey. Their name was the Andersons, and Eloise was so happy to meet them. The three children were ages four, seven, and nine. The little one,

Maggie, immediately grabbed Eloise's hand to show Eloise her bedroom and her collection of dolls. Andrew Jr., the seven-year-old, was a little shy but very polite and sweet. The oldest daughter, Elizabeth, was beautiful and tall with blue eyes and blond hair. The parents, Andrew Sr. and Nancy, were a very handsome and accomplished couple. They were both professors with PhDs in physics and psychology. The children's nanny was on vacation, so Eloise and the children had a good opportunity to get to know one another and have time together.

The Andersons were delighted by Eloise's loving nature and were happy to have her in their family. When they went for a walk around the property, all three children wanted to hold Eloise's hand. They loved her right away, and the whole family was making an effort to ease her pain from the loss of Roger. Eloise spent a few hours having dinner and talking with her new family that night, but soon after dinner she said good night. She needed to start preparing for classes the next day.

Before starting her preparations, she called her godparents at the hotel to let them know that she had received a warm welcome from her host family and she loved the children right away. "The children have such good manners," she said. "They are so polite. I'm happy, and I feel safe here with this family."

When Eloise finished talking with her godparents, she called her mom and dad. She chatted with her little brother Lui too. Her other brothers and sisters were all glad to hear from her too. Then she called the Strauss family and told them how she was doing. Everyone was pleased to hear from Eloise.

CHAPTER EIGHT

The next day, Eloise got up early. She was ready to begin her first day of school. She was so excited about meeting all her classmates and her three professors, who were the aces of the English language—the best in the field.

When Eloise arrived at the university, she found out that there were ten students in the class, six girls and four boys, and each one was from a different country. Everyone was new, and they were all meeting each other for the first time. It was fascinating to hear about everyone's different backgrounds. They would learn a lot about each other in the course of their first year together.

Then the professors took the students on a grand tour of the campus. The students were all in awe of the university grounds and the details of the program. They found out that they would be going on field trips throughout the year. Their classes were primarily English classes, but they would also be learning US history and so much more.

The schedule was Monday through Thursday from 8:00 a.m. to noon. They would be assigned homework every day that they could do individually or in a group. Eloise was happy to have a full schedule—keeping busy was exactly what she needed right then.

Eloise made friends with all her classmates right away. Her beauty and subdued sophistication intrigued everyone. As they got to know her, they found she was warmhearted and always smiling. She was also the most beautiful girl in the group. The boys had eyes only for her. Eloise continued to wear her engagement ring.

Before she left Brazil, Eloise told her parents and the Strauss family that she would wear her ring forever. Roger would be with her for the rest of her life. Her family and friends warned her that a ring on her finger would deter a man from approaching her. "I don't care," she said to them all. "I am not going to love another man as much as I loved Roger. He is irreplaceable. If, one day, I come to love another man, he will have to accept this fact. I will not take my ring off my finger to please anybody."

As the two weeks went by, Eloise's godparents were great company for her. They traveled to several places together: Washington, DC, Boston, and Philadelphia. At last, the day came when they would have to return home. Eloise was full of tears, but she knew that she had to stay and continue her journey.

The fall came, and several trips were planned for the students. The place Eloise most enjoyed visiting was New Hampshire to see the autumn leaves. The colors were absolutely breathtaking. She had never seen anything like it in her native Brazil. She was falling in love with the beauty of the United States, a country that received her with open arms.

She really enjoyed the American people as well. They were loving but independent, and the children were very focused on school and their daily duties. She also admired the attitude of *live and let live*.

Eloise realized that it was a great idea for her to come to the United States after all. She studied hard, and her progress in the language was outstanding. The only problem for Eloise was the nighttime. She cried every night and had trouble falling asleep. She was so tired during the day that sometimes she would fall asleep in class. Her professors were very understanding because they knew what Eloise was going through.

One of her professors approached her and kindly asked to have a private meeting with her and her other two professors. In the meeting, they spoke to Eloise about how she had been falling asleep in class. She told them she was having trouble sleeping at night, and the professors recommended that she meet with one of the university counselors. Eloise agreed to make an appointment.

The counselor was a psychologist, an older woman who had also lost a loved one. She asked Eloise to participate in three sessions to start. The counselor recommended that Eloise get plenty of exercise and stay active during the day, drink lots of water, and eat a balanced diet. Following the counselor's advice, Eloise started taking ballet lessons again. Over time, it worked wonders for her. She was ready for bed at 10:00 p.m. and fell asleep right away.

Eloise started going to church every Sunday for Mass. There she found the comfort and solace she was looking for. Eloise realized that there were other people in the world suffering from a loss or in hospitals. Many of them were much more distressed than Eloise. She began to work with children and families in need in the community. She had three days off from school every week, so she spent one of those days helping others in need. Little by little, she found herself feeling better.

In addition to volunteering and writing letters to her family, Eloise began to socialize with friends. Eloise would turn twenty-four that year; she was young and was starting to look forward to the new life ahead of her. She went out to restaurants and dancing with her new friends. They exchanged stories about foods from their countries. Whenever they could, they visited New York City to explore restaurants from around the world. As students, they didn't have much money for eating out or traveling, but they made the best of the chances they had to explore new cuisines.

Many university graduates and teachers asked Eloise to go out on dates with them, but she always refused. Then one of the girls in her group asked her to go on a double date with her in New York City. Eloise felt a little more comfortable with that arrangement, and she agreed to go. Her date was a French medical student. He was graduating and moving to New York City soon. The evening was pleasant, and as it came to an end, Pierre asked Eloise to go out with him again. She said, "Will we go out together with our other friends?"

"Of course," Pierre said, "if you prefer that. I promise to be nice to you and take you back to your home anytime you wish. You can trust me."

"I'll think about it," Eloise said. "Call me and I'll let you know."

When Eloise got home that night, Nancy asked how her date went and if she had a good time. Eloise was shy at first but finally admitted that Pierre had asked her to go out with him again. Nancy advised Eloise to think about it, but if she really wanted to get to know him better, she should suggest a walk in the park or another daytime outing. Eloise thanked Nancy for the great advice. She went out with Pierre again during the daytime. He was a great person and very focused on his career. In a few months, he would be moving to New York. Eloise felt a relief in a way—there was no pressure. They would just remain friends.

Eloise and Pierre went out a few times. The Anderson family was very pleased to see Eloise happy. Pierre had similar taste to Eloise in food, music, literature, and art—almost everything. They were a great match but only as friends. There was no romance between them. Pierre had a girlfriend in France, although he hadn't seen her in over a year.

He asked Eloise about her engagement ring, and she responded the same way she always did. She said firmly, "My fiancé died in a plane crash just before our wedding, and I still mourn my loss. Wearing the ring he gave me is a decision I have made. He is gone, but he will be in my heart forever."

"Eloise," he said calmly, "I admire you so much. You are very coura-geous, and I respect your feelings. I enjoy your company immensely, and if you wish to continue our friendship, I will be very happy." Eloise was happy to have Pierre's friendship; he was a gentleman. Her favorite family members had always been her little brother Lui and her father, so she liked having a male friend.

Life was good for Eloise now. She had a great group of friends and a daily routine that included ballet and exercise. She enjoyed her classes and had a very good relationship with her host family. She kept in touch with her family back home by writing letters.

Through some mutual friends, Eloise met another Brazilian student who was from Rio. Her name was Lucia, and she lived in Philadelphia. Lucia was the same age as Eloise and came from a similar background. Lucia didn't have a scholarship; she was paying for school in full. She had a car, so she would often come to see Eloise or pick up Eloise and bring her to Philly, because Eloise did not drive.

Eloise mostly took public transportation, and her host family would take her places as much as possible. If Eloise decided to learn to drive, she could get a license with her temporary status as a student.

On New Year's Eve, Eloise got to see snow for the first time in the United States. She had gone on a ski trip with Roger in Argentina once, but she only played in the snow and didn't learn how to ski. Now she was determined to learn. Her group would be going on a skiing field trip to Vermont later in January, and Lucia would be going along with them. She was excited and looking forward to a great adventure on the slopes. She wanted to learn cross-country skiing first. The Andersons helped her pick the proper ski clothing. The group would rent the skis at the slope.

They stayed in a chalet reserved just for them for the week. Each day, breakfast and dinner were prepared for them. Eloise fell in love with Vermont. It was just beautiful in the snow. The beauty was tinged with sadness, though, because the snow reminded her of Roger.

As the days went by, Eloise's sadness increased. Eventually the memories became so overwhelming that she had to take time off from being with her friends and retreated off by herself. Eloise didn't know what to say to her friends, so she just made an excuse about why she wanted to be on her own for a while. Luckily, Lucia was someone Eloise could talk to. Since Lucia was from Brazil, Eloise told her about Roger right away, and now Lucia knew how to console Eloise.

Eloise felt shy and a little embarrassed when she could not hold back her tears in front of people. She always said it was because she missed her family a great deal and it would be a while before she got used to being away from them.

When the week came to an end, the group returned to school. Everyone was talking about the trip, sharing pictures, and sending pictures home to their families.

Soon springtime came, and there was another big trip on the schedule. This one was to Washington, DC, for the cherry blossom festival. It was a magical experience for the students. They got to visit the Smithsonian Museum, the White House, and many historical sites.

CHAPTER NINE

Eloise was doing well in school—so well that she was considering staying in school for one more year. If she did, she would get more credits and better job offers either in Brazil or in the United States if she decided to stay. One thing was for sure; she would go home to see her family, whom she missed so much. Her phone bills were high from calling her family every week. Her parents told her to call them once a month, and they would call her once a month. Roger's parents would also call once a month.

Eloise was still not emotionally ready for any kind of romance. She was intrigued by Mr. and Mrs. Anderson's relationship. Eloise had been so busy with her own life that she had not noticed it before. For one, they did not share a bedroom, and Andrew traveled so much that his wife was constantly alone. Andrew was a very good-looking man; in fact, Eloise thought he looked like Roger. There was a world of difference in their character, though. Roger had been so warm and loving. Eloise imagined that Andrew and Nancy married for many other reasons besides love.

They met when they were in college, and they were both eighteen years old. They finished college, got married, and started a family a few years later as they pursued their PhDs. They both came from well-to-do families. They went to the best colleges and universities in the country and were high achievers in their fields. Now they were in their late thirties, which was still young to be so detached from each other. She admired them for their achievements, but where was the love? If it existed at all, nobody could see it.

Andrew and Nancy were distant and formal with their children, so the children developed a bond with Eloise, which she loved. Still, it was strange for her to realize that they preferred her company and her love over their parents'. The children had beautiful clothes, expensive toys, and trips to Disneyland, but the connection with their parents was not there, and they were not happy and hardly smiled.

Eloise felt comfortable with the family. They were very caring as far as she was concerned. The children would eat early, and later Mr. and Mrs. Anderson would have dinner with Eloise. She wondered if they wanted her with them so that they would have someone else to talk to. They always talked about business and similar subjects—not the conversation of a loving couple.

Sometimes Eloise felt very sorry for those children. The hugs and love they received came from Eloise. She knew that something was wrong with Andrew and Nancy's marriage. She guessed that they would not stay together when their children went away to college. Andrew, when he was not traveling, was seldom at home. He would go out practically every night, and he never took the children on an outing. Nancy was always busy with her own business.

Andrew used to drive Eloise in the evenings when she needed a ride. One night, Andrew told her that he needed to talk to her privately. Eloise had no idea why, but agreed to talk to him on her way over to a friend's house. He stopped the car in front of her friend's house. "Eloise, there is something I want to tell you," he said. "My wife and I are going to get a divorce. The children don't know yet. We thought it would be appropriate to tell you first. We are planning on having a meeting with the kids this weekend when they are at home." Eloise was not surprised.

"I'm sorry to hear that, Mr. Anderson," she said. "Don't worry. I won't say anything to the children."

"Please call me Andrew," he said. "Eloise, I admire you so much. You are beautiful, and you are so loving with the children. I know that one day you'll have a family of your own, and you'll be a great mother."

"Thank you," Eloise said, flattered by his comments. Andrew looked so sad. It was the first time Eloise had seen him showing so much emotion. "Maybe you and Nancy will come to change your minds," she said. "You have a great family, and your children are so loving. Maybe you just need some time off to be with your family. Is there any hope of that?"

"No," Andrew said, shaking his head. "We're just not right for each other. We do have three lovely children, and it is so sad to see how the tension between us makes them unhappy. My wife and I have no affection or love for one another, and it's been that way for a long time. We drifted so far apart; now there is no way back. After our son was born, we decided to have separate bedrooms, and we haven't made love since our youngest child was born." Eloise never imagined she would hear such a confession from Andrew, who always seemed so reserved. He went on to say, "We didn't conceive our youngest daughter out of love; it was just one night when we both had been drinking and felt desperate for affection. The marriage was over before she was even born. Still, she is our loving daughter. It pains me to see my children so unhappy. When we get divorced, we will all be better for it." Then Andrew looked at Eloise and took her hands in his. "Please, Eloise," he begged, "do not leave the family. I would like to have joint custody of my children, but I don't want to take them away from their mother."

"Would you have them live with you, if your wife allowed it?"

"Yes, yes, yes," he said with conviction. "I am even going to cut down on my traveling to spend more time with them." Then he looked down, somewhat defeated. "But I know how the law is. Primary custody will be granted to their mother. I would have to fight for it, and that is something I would never do. It's against my principles, and it would hurt my children so much. After we tell the children, I will stay for a few more days to reassure them that I am not abandoning them. Then I will move out temporarily while my wife looks for a new house. I will always be a presence in their lives, even if we are not living under the same roof full time."

"They are great kids," Eloise said.

"They love you so much," Andrew said. "You brought laughter and sunshine into their lives. I am grateful that God sent you to our home. I wish you the very best, and I promise to always be in touch." Andrew asked Eloise to keep the conversation between the two of them, and she agreed. Andrew had been so honest and heartfelt as he spoke. Usually he seemed so somber and serious. Eloise liked seeing him in a different light. He was a good father and a very good man.

Over the next few days, Eloise was dreading the children's reaction when they heard their parents were getting divorced. Only their older daughter was old enough to understand what a divorce was. When the day came for the family gathering, Eloise chose to be away for the weekend to let them have their privacy.

When she returned, Nancy asked to speak to her privately. Eloise pretended not to know anything, since she had promised Andrew that she would keep their conversation private. Mrs. Anderson said very matter-of-factly that they would be getting a divorce. "I am sorry to hear that," Eloise said.

"Don't be," Nancy said. "The children reacted very positively to the news. Nothing much will change here. Andrew is entitled to the house, as it is part of his deal with the university. I will be moving out with the children. I am actually happy to move. I never liked this house." She looked around the room disdainfully. Then she went on to say, "We will begin to look for a new house in the next few weeks. We will stay here for now, and Andrew will rent an apartment until we are ready to move. I hope you will remain with us. The children really care about you." Eloise thanked her, and the conversation ended there.

One thing about the conversation with Nancy stayed with Eloise. As Nancy spoke, she was completely emotionless. Was she so hurt that she didn't want to show it, or was she actually uncaring? Eloise was puzzled about these two people who had lived for so long as husband and wife. Maybe they never had any real passion or love for each other.

Two months had passed since the divorce was announced. Andrew had taken an apartment in town, and Nancy didn't seem to be in a hurry to move. One day Eloise got a call from Andrew. He asked if she would meet with him for a private conversation. He suggested they take a drive out of town and have lunch together. Eloise was a little intrigued. Maybe he wanted to find out from her how things were at home, but she knew he was in constant contact with his children and that they were visiting him regularly. Why did he want to see her? She agreed to meet him at his office, and then they would go out of town for lunch.

Once they were in the car, Eloise felt awkward. It seemed like a date. Eloise hadn't seen Andrew for two months, and he had transformed. He seemed happy. His smile made him look younger and more handsome. She thought of how much he reminded her of Roger. They were both tall with blue eyes and a beautiful smile. Eloise realized the marriage had been destroying Andrew. Now he was a new man. They talked about music and art and discovered they had many shared interests. They both had a fun afternoon.

"The reason I asked you to lunch," Andrew said, "is because I wanted to thank you for being you. You have been an angel in my children's lives. I hope to be able to do something for you in the future. If you decide to stay in this area after you complete school, I will help you in any way I can."

"Thank you," Eloise said. She was glad to have his support.

It was almost five o'clock when they returned to town. Eloise had forgotten her glasses in Andrew's office. She picked up her glasses and was saying good-bye when Andrew gave her a warm hug. She suddenly felt compelled to kiss him on the cheek. He kissed her cheek back, and then they kissed each other on the lips. They paused for a moment and looked into each other's eyes and then kissed again, more passionately. Then Eloise pulled away and took a few steps back. She realized her terrible mistake. She knew they were two people in great need of love and affection. Andrew was not in love with her, and she was not in love with him. "I enjoyed the kiss," she said, "but I can't do this. You and your wife are not yet divorced. You are still going to counseling, and you might even get back together. Let's not get involved now. We both know it is not going to work."

"Eloise," he said, "I have been in love with you for a long time. You are not the reason for my breakup with my wife. It was broken long before you came to our lives. So please do not feel guilty. As for going back to my marriage? There is not a chance in the world. My wife and I are so wrong for each other. I haven't been happy like this since my college days."

"After Roger's death, I never loved anyone else or even had an intimate affair with any other man. I miss it," Eloise said. She had almost thought she would never find that love again. Andrew knew she was vulnerable.

"Can I see you again?" he asked. Eloise had a private phone line, and he knew her number. "Can I call you?"

"I need some time to think about it," Eloise said. "I'll call you when I'm ready." They kissed again good night. A huge sexual desire came rushing into Eloise's body, making her tremble.

That night, Eloise could not sleep. She could not imagine having an amorous relationship with Andrew. How would she handle that? What would Nancy think? How would the children react? No, it couldn't happen. She prayed silently, "My God, please help me here. I am so helpless. I need to be strong. I do not want an affair just because I am in such great need of a man's love and affection."

A few days passed, and Nancy asked Eloise to have a private conversation with her after the kids had gone to bed. Eloise felt a prick of anxiety, but she agreed to speak to Nancy.

"Eloise," Nancy said, "I hired a detective to follow my husband when he traveled to California. I discovered that he is having an affair. He has a secret hideaway where he meets his mistress. I am going to travel there to confront him." Eloise wondered why Nancy was telling her so many intimate details. She didn't know what to say, so she just listened quietly. Nancy went on, "My husband and I were separated for many years, but he only accepted the separation because he had someone else in his life."

"Mrs. Anderson," Eloise said, "you have my deepest sympathy, but you and your children will be over all these troubles soon. As for me, I am here as your guest. I will do my best to make you comfortable with having me here as you go through a difficult time."

"Please," Nancy said, "just tell me anything you hear from Andrew. I'm not going to allow him to take the children on vacations unless he stops seeing that woman." Eloise refused to respond to Nancy's threats to her husband—after all, it wasn't any of her business.

A few weeks later, Andrew called Eloise. "I know you said to wait and that you would call me," he said, "but it has been weeks, and I'm dying to see you again." She hesitated but then agreed to meet him in his office during the day. At the office, he told her that he would be moving out of state in a couple of months because he preferred to work in California for a while. Eloise thought, *So, it may be true about the other woman.* Then Andrew said, "I have to tell you something. I think it is important for you to know that I had someone in my life for about two years. We no longer see each other. My wife knew about her, but she did not want to divorce. She told me she couldn't care less, as long we stayed married. It was not for the children's sake; it was for the money and for social reasons. It was hard for me to be alone for so long. I needed love, and I searched for it. This affair was good for a time, but I knew I was fooling myself to think it was true love." Eloise said that Nancy told her about the affair and that she was going to have a detective follow him. "Let her," Andrew said. "It doesn't matter anymore. I will get a divorce with or without her signature, and I will spend more time with my children. I'm going to bring them to California for the summer."

Eloise was relieved to hear his confession. She liked Andrew and didn't want to stop spending time with him. The children visited him every other weekend, and sometimes they would invite Eloise to come on an outing. They visited the children's grandparents in their beautiful home by the Hudson River, went picnicking, walked in the woods, and watched movies. Andrew's parents loved Eloise and always asked her to return to visit them again. Andrew and Eloise developed a beautiful friendship after he and Nancy filed for divorce.

The children were always asking to go out with their father, and Nancy actually felt relived to be able to spend more time alone. Eloise and Andrew were developing mutual admiration and attraction. One weekend, at Andrew's parents' house, he asked Eloise to go out to dinner with him that night. Eloise said yes, and he took her to dinner in Manhattan at very well-known French restaurant. It was Andrew's favorite. They had a great dinner and then went to a Broadway show. They ended the night drinking cocktails at another bistro. It was there that Andrew confessed to Eloise that he was in love with her. "I feel very comfortable in your company, Andrew," Eloise said. "But I don't know what to do. It is a rather awkward situation. Your children and your wife will all think that we have been having an affair and that was the reason for your divorce. I will be called a home-wrecker. It is impossible for you and I to be together. Don't you see?"

"Eloise," he said, "I am going to California soon. I have already arranged for my children to come and spend the summer with me. Would you consider coming with us? We would have more time together to discuss the future. Please say yes."

"Yes," Eloise said with a smile, "but I must consult with Nancy and tell her that I will be going to help you with the children while you are at work. It will be like a summer job babysitting for me."

Nancy agreed to let Eloise go on the trip. It was planned for the second week of June through the end of August. Nancy was preparing to move with the children before school started in September.

Eloise had decided to stay in the United States for another year, but she wasn't sure if she would be staying in the Andersons' home. She wanted to get an apartment with her friend Lucia, who also wanted to continue her studies for another year. It would be good to have a friend for a roommate and to be more independent.

Eloise was attracted to Andrew, but deep down in her heart she knew it was because Andrew reminded her of Roger. She felt the need to be loved again. Before they left for California, she told Andrew how she felt, knowing it was a risk to compare him to the fiancé she had lost. He understood, though, and said he was aware of her feelings and willing to take a chance.

They made plans to go out together in New York City. Andrew wanted to book a hotel room so they wouldn't have to drive home late at night. Eloise agreed, as long as he booked two rooms. She was not ready to be intimate with Andrew. He understood and respected her wishes. They went out for dinner and dancing and had a great evening. Andrew was a gentleman, and he escorted Eloise to her room, kissing her good night. They would have breakfast together in the morning.

Eloise was slowly falling in love with Andrew, but she was being cautious. She knew there were many problems they would have to face if they became serious about each other. She knew she had to use common sense.

The next morning, they had a long, leisurely breakfast together, talking about their upcoming trip. Andrew was going to travel to California first to get some work done and prepare everything for their arrival. He had rented a beautiful house near his office in Palo Alto. It had a pool and a maid who would do the cooking and look after their every need.

"Eloise," he said, "I'm so happy you'll be staying with us. I really trust you with my children, and we're going to have a great time together. I already have some trips planned—to Yosemite and Disneyland."

"That sounds great, Andrew," Eloise said.

"I'd also like to take you to San Francisco for a couple of days, so we can spend a weekend together—just the two of us. It's one of my favorite cities in the world, and I would love to show you around."

"I'd like that," Eloise said, taking a sip of her coffee.

"Eloise," Andrew said as he moved closer and spoke in a low voice. "I want to be intimate with you. It is up to you, though. I understand if you don't want to be with me, and that won't change things for me. I have always admired your qualities—your poise, grace, sophistication, and impeccable manners. You are a joy to be with. I imagine that your fiancé admired and loved you very much."

Eloise didn't know what to say. She thought about what her godmother told her when she lost Roger. *He will be in heaven, as a star in the sky, looking out for you. Roger would want you to find happiness again.* In her prayers, she always thanked God and her guardian angel for guiding her and protecting her. Life had been good to her. She knew she had to help others who were in despair out of gratitude for all the grace she had received.

Sometimes she would say to God, "One day, dear God, I want to have a child to love and care for." She had this thought when she was with Roger; although she knew they would never have a biological child together, she was willing to share her love with an adopted child.

That morning, Eloise told Andrew more about Roger. She described how they met and talked about the four years of glorious love they shared. She told Andrew that they couldn't have a biological child but didn't go into detail. Andrew just listened. Eloise was enchanted by Andrew's character. He was a true gentleman.

CHAPTER TEN

The day came when Andrew would leave for California. The children were so excited about the trip. Nancy stayed out of it, not once showing any emotion over their excitement or the fact that they were leaving. As usual, she was like a rock. Eloise sometimes wondered what was on her mind. Was she happy that she was going to be alone? Was she angry she was not going? They had come to have fewer and fewer conversations.

A couple of days before the trip, Nancy called Eloise aside for a chat. She asked her to take note of Andrew's actions. "I would like to know if his girlfriend comes to visit him," Nancy said, "and whether she spends the night at the house. It would be inappropriate for him to do that, and I still could take away Andrew's right to spend time with the kids." Eloise was shocked to hear Nancy's request.

"The reason I am going on the trip," Eloise said, "is to spend more time with the children. After all, I will be moving out in the fall, so this is our last opportunity to have some time together."

"Yes, I know," Nancy said. "But it would be a favor to me if you let me know what happens in California. I could get a better settlement from my husband if he wants to get married again, and I need to have all the ammunition now, before the divorce is final."

Eloise nodded, but she didn't promise Nancy anything.

A few days later, Eloise and the children left New Jersey to go to California with Andrew. Both Eloise and the children had never been to California before, and they were all excited for this new adventure. Andrew met them at the airport and drove them to Palo Alto. When they arrived at the house, Eloise was enchanted. It was huge—an absolute mansion. There were six bedrooms, five baths, a guesthouse, a beautiful pool with a Jacuzzi, a maid's quarters, and more. The housekeeper and the driver were a delightful older couple with very distinct Spanish accents. All the cooking would be done by a younger woman who was an expert chef. Andrew had hired all of them for the duration of their stay in California.

It was still early, so Eloise and the kids decided to have lunch by the pool and relax for the rest of the day. Another professor at the university told Andrew about a country club where the children could meet others their age. Andrew brought them there the next day for lunch. They went to the pool, and the kids met several other children. They played games together in the pool and received invitations to a few birthday parties.

Andrew had planned a weekend trip to San Francisco for himself and Eloise. He wanted so much to be alone with her, and she was also anxious to have some time alone with him. He booked them two rooms at a very famous hotel overlooking beautiful San Francisco Bay. The first evening there, Andrew took Eloise to see the opera *La Traviata*. Eloise had been to the opera before, but this was the first time she really enjoyed herself. The story was sad and romantic. Afterward, they went for a nightcap at the hotel bar. As they sipped their drinks, they shared about themselves, and Eloise felt even closer to Andrew than before. He escorted Eloise to her room and was about to give her a gentle kiss good night. Eloise noticed the look of surprise on his face when she invited him inside. As soon as the door was shut behind them, Eloise grabbed Andrew and gave him a passionate kiss. He kissed back just as passionately; he was excited that they were about to share their first night together.

Eloise grabbed him by the tie and pulled him over to the bed. Then she untied his tie and slipped it off. As she unbuttoned his shirt, he unzipped her dress, both kissing each other hungrily on the lips, face, and neck the entire time. Eloise ran her hands over Andrew's bare chest as he caressed her neck. He slipped off her dress, unhooked her bra, and soon he had stripped off Eloise's underwear, leaving her completely naked. Eloise craved Andrew so much that she didn't feel shy at all.

Their uninhibited lovemaking was extraordinary. It was as if they had waited for this moment forever, like a deep thirst was being quenched. They did not stop making love until the early hours of the morning, when they finally collapsed into a deep sleep.

Hours later, when they woke up, Eloise could hardly believe what had happened. He got up and whispered tenderly, "My beautiful girl, my delightful woman, my princess, you seduced me. I promise you I would have gone to my own room and cried there for you, but I am delighted that you wanted me as much as I wanted you."

"Hush, hush," Eloise whispered back. "I am not letting you go. I want every part of you in my life now."

"Yes," Andrew said. "That's what I hoped for, because that's what I want too. Let's not worry about anything else right now, my darling. I told the children we would be away three nights, but let's stay away for four at least. I need another night with you before we join our children again." She was delighted by what had come out of Andrew's mouth, *our children.*

"The only thing on my mind is enjoying every minute with you," Eloise said.

The next three nights were a utopia as Eloise and Andrew shared their dreams for the future, promised to love each other, and imagined their lives together. Andrew told Eloise that he had no fear and was prepared to fight for his love. He had never lived such an adventurous life before, and Eloise was the most sensuous and loving woman he'd ever been with. Eloise had loved Roger very much, and he had been her first lover, but it was Roger who brought out her womanhood.

During the day, they went on sightseeing trips all over the city. They had great fun exploring San Francisco, but they could hardly wait to get back to their love nest in the evening. Andrew had kept both rooms in case he was being followed or spied on by his ex-wife.

For the rest of their time in California, Andrew and Eloise decided to spend the weekdays with the kids, but for at least three evenings a week, they would be alone together. It was easy to arrange most of the time. The servants went to the guesthouse in the evening, and, in any case, they were very discrete. Andrew and Eloise also went on trips with the children. They took them to Disneyland for four nights. The children loved every minute of it, and so did Eloise. Next they went to Hollywood for the thrill of being in the world of movies and stars.

As they walked down Hollywood Boulevard, a man approached Eloise. "Excuse me, miss," he said. "I'm a talent scout, and I'm wondering if you ever considered a career in film." Eloise laughed, but the children were cheering her on.

"You could be famous!" Elizabeth called out.

"You could be a movie star!" Maggie added.

Eloise laughed again and said, "That's the last thing I have on my mind to do." Although she had wanted to be an actress when she was younger, it no longer interested her. "I don't want to be an actress," she said. "I have other plans for my future." Then she laughed again, and Andrew laughed along with her. "I'm just here as a fan," she said.

The next trip the family took was to San Diego. They went to the famous San Diego Zoo and went on the safari tour. Then they went to the beach, where they watched the sea lions sunbathing on the rocks and did the same. The whole family drove further south then, across the border to Tijuana, Mexico.

When they returned to Palo Alto, they were exhausted. They needed a vacation to rest after their vacation. Eloise didn't feel well, and she figured it was probably because she'd been eating out too much. Since she had been born premature, she had a very sensitive constitution. Her parents had raised her on all-natural foods, and as an adult, she had to choose what to eat carefully. She couldn't drink much alcohol or eat too many spicy or processed foods.

She realized she had to be more selective about what she ate in restaurants. In her country, it was a simple matter of saying she was always on a diet. She couldn't have sauces or hot peppers, although she loved spicy food. The cuisine in Brazil was the best in the world for her—it was so varied and fresh. Anywhere she went out to eat, she could find great food. Eloise had been shy about mentioning to Andrew and others that she had a delicate condition, so she ignored it and ate everything. Now she was feeling the consequences. During dinner with Andrew and the children, she explained that from now on she had to be careful and avoid eating things that could make her sick. She had a conversation with their cook about her diet too. The cook agreed to make Eloise's diet a priority.

Time was speeding by. They had been in California for six weeks already. There were only two weeks left before they had to return to New Jersey. They spent most of the time in Palo Alto, enjoying all the local places, going shopping, and lying around the pool. The children had made friends their ages, so they invited them over to have barbecues around the pool, watch movies, and play together.

Andrew took Eloise away to Monterey County for a four-day trip, just the two of them. Eloise fell in love with Caramel and Big Sur. One night, they were relaxing in their hotel room in Big Sur when Andrew said, "Eloise, will you move to California with me?"

"Andrew," Eloise said gently, "it has been a year and a half since I left my home and my family. I like California a lot, but I need to focus on finishing my studies by the end of year. Then I want to go home for Christmas."

"I know," Andrew said, "but don't you love it here? I just want to be with you, Eloise. Please say yes."

"First I have to go home for Christmas. Let's wait until I'm back to decide. I'm still not sure if California is the place I want to be," she said.

"I understand," Andrew said, "but I wish you would say yes."

"I would love to be with you," Eloise said, "but you are still involved in this divorce. I think you should wait until the divorce is finalized before starting a serious relationship with me. Please, let's give ourselves time."

"Okay. I know you're right," Andrew said reluctantly. "I'm just afraid of losing you."

"You're not going to lose me," Eloise said, putting her arms around him and holding him tightly. "I'll come see you whenever possible. In the meantime, we just have to wait to see what the future brings."

CHAPTER ELEVEN

Despite watching her diet, Eloise was still not feeling well. She constantly felt dizzy and had a lack of appetite. She finally decided to go see a doctor, and Andrew arranged an appointment for her with a physician at a medical clinic at Stanford. Andrew took her to the appointment. He'd found her a female doctor, so Eloise felt comfortable. The examination took about an hour, and tests were done. The next day, Eloise went back for a follow-up appointment. "I have the results of the tests," the doctor said, "and I have some important news to share with you. Eloise, you're pregnant."

Eloise was shocked and scared, but after a moment, she realized she should not be surprised. She and Andrew had been so careless! Before now, she had only been with Roger, who was not able to get her pregnant. She had never needed to use any sort of contraception before. She felt so silly. How in the world did she not expect to get pregnant with Andrew? "Are you sure?" Eloise asked the doctor hopefully. "Could this be a mistake?"

"It's no mistake," the doctor said. "You are pregnant."

"I'd like to come back to see you again tomorrow," Eloise said. The doctor said that was fine and told her to make an appointment with the receptionist. Andrew was waiting for Eloise in the waiting room. When she saw him, she started to cry. "My God, Andrew," she said, "I'm pregnant."

Andrew gave her a guilty look and said quickly, "Eloise what are you going to do?"

"Andrew, please!" Eloise said, "What do you mean, what am *I* going to do? Don't you mean, what are *we* going to do? We have to make a decision together—not just me alone."

"Yes, Eloise," Andrew said. "I am sorry. That came out wrong, and I apologize." Eloise crossed her arms. She felt confused and frightened. "Please," Andrew said, "let's go out for dinner later—just the two of us— and we'll talk." Then he added, "Don't worry, Eloise. I am here for you." They embraced, but Eloise still felt worried.

She called her friend Lucia, whom she had planned to be roommates with during the coming school year. "Lucia," Eloise said, "please get us the apartment as soon as possible. I want to move out of the Andersons' home as soon as I get back to New Jersey." Eloise explained that she had decided to cut her vacation in California short. Lucia didn't ask why it was so urgent.

"I already found a place not far from the university," Lucia said.

"Great," Eloise replied. "Please rent it immediately. I'll be there in three days."

That evening, she and Andrew went out for dinner as he had suggested. The mood was somber, and they picked at their food, hardly eating. Eloise was quiet with worry, because she didn't know what would happen next. Andrew tried to comfort her, but Eloise still felt uncertain. All she knew was that she needed Andrew to be on her side, supporting her. She had so many plans for her future, and now everything was going to change. How would her family react? Should she go back to Brazil immediately?

Andrew tried to be soothing, but he didn't have much to say. He was in love with Eloise, but she wasn't sure whether he was willing to take full responsibility for the situation. She could stay in California. Would this change anything between them? They would have to hide the pregnancy from his wife until the divorce was final; otherwise she would raise hell, most likely accusing them of having an affair before he filed for divorce.

"Will you make me a reservation for a flight back to New Jersey?" Eloise said.

"Yes, of course," he said. "Why do you want to go back now?"

"I need to go and get my thoughts together," Eloise said. "My friend Lucia will meet me at the airport, and then I'm going to move out of the house and into an apartment with her."

"Okay," Andrew said. "I'll fly back to New Jersey with the children the following week, and then I'll stay there in New Jersey so I can be close to you." Hearing this made Eloise feel better. Andrew was making an effort to help her.

When Eloise arrived in New Jersey, Lucia was anxious to know what was happening with her dear friend. It took a couple of days before Eloise was ready to tell Lucia that she was pregnant. When she did, Lucia didn't ask any questions; all she said was, "I'll find you a good doctor near here."

Lucia helped Eloise find a female doctor whom she liked. The doctor told Eloise that her pregnancy was six weeks along. Eloise knew that she had to prepare herself for a lot of changes in her life, but she wanted to wait until Andrew returned before doing anything. She was anxious about the future, but she knew she would love this child dearly. She hadn't planned on getting pregnant, but she was determined to be a great mother no matter what.

A couple of days later, Eloise woke up in the early morning with a cramp in her abdomen. She curled up in a ball, writhing in pain. It was so unbearable that she cried out, sweat beading on her forehead and tears running down her cheeks. It was very early, but when Lucia heard Eloise cry out, she rushed into her bedroom. "What's wrong?" she asked.

"Please," Eloise said, "call the doctor. I feel like I am dying."

Lucia called the doctor she had found for Eloise. "Take her to the hospital immediately," the doctor ordered. Lucia helped Eloise get out of bed and into her clothes. Then she drove Eloise to the nearest emergency room. The doctor arrived at the hospital shortly after Eloise was admitted.

"I think I'm bleeding," Eloise told the doctor. Lucia was by her side, holding her hand.

"There is a problem. You may be having a miscarriage," the doctor said. As soon as she spoke those words, Eloise fell back into the hospital bed and fainted.

The doctor was right—Eloise lost the baby. She stayed in the hospital for a few days. Lucia was such a good friend; she stayed with her the entire time. Eloise called Andrew from the hospital.

"How are you?" Andrew said. "I was worried after not hearing from you for a few days."

"Andrew," Eloise said, "I'm in the hospital. I had a miscarriage. The doctors don't know why. I was six or seven weeks pregnant."

"Oh, Eloise, I am so sorry," Andrew said. "Are you okay?"

"I'm still recovering in the hospital," Eloise said. "Lucia is with me. She's been the best friend I could ever hope for. I'm okay."

"I want to come see you," Andrew said.

"No," Eloise said softly. "Don't rush the children back now. Stay with them a little longer, until it is time for them to come back for school."

"Are you sure?" Andrew asked.

"Yes," Eloise said. "We will see each other when you arrive. I moved to an apartment with Lucia. It's lovely there. I'm continuing my studies until winter break in December, when I'll go home to Brazil to see my family for Christmas." Now Eloise could hear Andrew sobbing quietly on the other end of the phone.

"I will call you as soon as I get back home," he whispered.

"Andrew, I want to thank you for your support through all of this," Eloise said. "We'll talk soon." She could hear Andrew shuddering as he cried.

As the days passed, Eloise started to feel better, and she resumed classes. In her prayers, she thanked God for taking care of her. As soon as Andrew got back from California, he called Eloise. They went out to dinner to talk. Andrew told Eloise that Nancy was finally accepting the fact that the divorce was a sure thing no matter how much dirt she tried to throw at him. According to the law, the divorce didn't have to be mutually agreed upon for it to be valid.

Still, Nancy was trying to lure Andrew back. She invited him over for dinner, and when he got there, he realized she'd sent the children away to sleep over at friends' houses for the night. He wanted to remain friendly with her for the children's sake, so he didn't complain. During dinner, she spiked his drink, getting him drunk. She convinced him to get into bed with her, but then the joke was on her. He was too drunk to perform. It was a ridiculous situation.

Andrew was so drunk he could barely walk and was definitely too drunk to drive. He had no choice but to spend the rest of the night at the house. He was miserable the whole night. Later, Nancy's attorney claimed that Andrew wanted to spend the night with her. It became another messy, complicated issue he had to deal with. Eloise had enough. She didn't want to be involved in the drama between Andrew and Nancy. She told Andrew that they should not see each other for a while.

CHAPTER TWELVE

Lucia introduced Eloise to several of her friends. One of them was Yara, a woman who worked for a Brazilian firm located in New York City. Just before Christmas, Yara called Eloise and told her about an international company located in New York that was looking for a Portuguese and Spanish language interpreter. Eloise thanked Yara and sent her résumé to the company. They asked her to come to their office for a personal interview.

Lucia went with Eloise to New York. They decided to make the most of the opportunity by spending a few days in the Big Apple. At the interview, Eloise met the company president. He was very impressed by her education, poise, and communication skills. She told him about her upcoming trip to Brazil for Christmas vacation. "I won't be available until February or March of next year, when I get back to the US," she said.

"We want you for the job," he said, "and we are willing to wait until you return."

Eloise was thrilled. She had found a job! She was starting her career. Then she thought about Andrew. He was back in California, where he had returned after finalizing his divorce. He was sad that Eloise had decided not to see him again. Now it seemed life was taking them away from each other.

Now she was focused on her new life, making new plans and new friends, which didn't include getting involved in a relationship. She felt better for it.

Eloise felt healthy and was looking forward to seeing her family again. December came quickly, and soon Eloise would be leaving for Brazil. One night she got a call from Andrew asking her to meet him. She hesitated at first but agreed to see him the night before she flew to Rio.

When Andrew arrived at the apartment to pick her up, Lucia opened the door. Upon seeing him, Lucia was struck by how gorgeous Andrew was. He was carrying a bouquet of beautiful roses for Eloise. Then he surprised Lucia by handing her a box of bonbons. "These are for you," he said.

"Oh, that's so kind," Lucia said. "Eloise will be ready in a few minutes." While Andrew waited for Eloise, they chatted, and she was struck by his charm. She was not surprised that Eloise had fallen in love with him.

"Would you like to come with us to dinner?" Andrew asked.

"Thank you, but I have other plans for the evening," Lucia said. She smiled; Andrew was certainty a gentleman. Eloise emerged from her room, looking beautiful as ever. Andrew gave her a hug and a kiss. Eloise felt a little faint. It had been a long time since she had seen Andrew, and as he put his arms around her, she felt overcome by emotions.

That evening, they had a wonderful time together. As he was dropping her off at her apartment, Andrew said, "Eloise, can I take you to the airport tomorrow?"

"Yes," Eloise said. "That's very kind of you."

The next morning, Andrew arrived early to pick up Eloise. They would stop for lunch on the way to the airport. Then they would have time to talk and be together before her 8:00 p.m. flight. After they had been driving for a while, Andrew said, "Eloise, I'm so sorry for what you had to go through. I feel terrible about it. I am so sorry I caused you so much pain."

"No, Andrew," Eloise said. "We both made a mistake. It wasn't only your fault." They were quiet for a moment, and then Eloise said, "I want you to know that if I hadn't had a miscarriage, I would have gone through with the pregnancy. I did love you when we made love, so please don't feel guilty. You helped me through my grief and sadness. You showed me that I needed to love again and be loved again. I thank you for that." Tears began to run down Eloise's face, and then Andrew was crying too.

"I loved you too. I still do," Andrew said.

"With you, the beauty of love came back into my life and into my heart."

"Eloise," Andrew said, "I want to be together with you again. I miss you so much."

"It's impossible for us to have a future together," Eloise said. "Your children would never understand. They would always think I was the cause of your divorce, and they would never forgive me."

"No," Andrew said, "they love you so much."

"Yes," Eloise said, "and I want them to remember me as a loving person who came into their lives. Please try to understand my perspective."

"It is so painful to think that we'll never be together," Andrew said.

"I wish you love and happiness always," Eloise said, "but we must remain friends—just friends."

"It hurts to admit it, but I know you are right," Andrew said.

Only time could heal their broken hearts. Andrew was moving to California and signing a three-year contract with his firm. Eloise was off to Brazil for a month, and when she returned, she would most likely be in New York for another year. If she decided to stay in the United States, she would want to go to California because she loved the mountains and the warm weather.

CHAPTER THIRTEEN

Eloise arrived in Brazil early the next morning. A huge crowd was at the airport to greet her—nearly her entire family. They were all eager to see Eloise after she had been gone almost two years. She was amazed to see how much her little brother Lui had grown. He was older but still the loving brother Eloise so adored. Her godparents were so happy to see their goddaughter recovered from her grief and adjusted to a new life without her beloved Roger.

Being back home brought back memories of Roger, and tears still came to Eloise's eyes just thinking about the man she would always love. Roger's parents waited a few days after Eloise's return to allow her time to visit with her family, but finally they called Eloise and invited her to get together with them. Eloise was eager to see them. When she went to their house, the Strausses told Eloise that they had created a trust fund for Eloise as per Roger's wishes. "We're going to come visit you in New York," Mrs. Strauss said. "We are planning a long trip for ourselves." They would visit New York first, then their beloved homeland, Austria, and from there they would visit other parts of Europe. They expected to be gone for about a year.

Eloise told them about her own plans to stay in New York another year. "We will always stay in touch," Eloise said. It was hard for them to talk without mentioning Roger, but the deep wound of loss had subsided. Roger had been the Strauss's only son, which made it especially painful to lose him. This was why they wanted to go back to Austria. They would connect with relatives there.

"Can I come visit you in Austria?" Eloise asked. "Roger told me so much about it and how much he loved it there. I want to see Salzburg, his second-favorite city after Vienna."

"Of course you can come visit," Mr. Strauss said. "It would be a pleasure to have you."

"Please let me know when you have settled there," Eloise said, "so I can plan a trip."

"We would love that," Mr. Strauss said.

Then Mrs. Strauss asked Eloise to help them with something that had been too difficult for them to do. They had not been in Roger's apartment since his death. They could not bear the idea of going through his personal belongings. Eloise was hesitant, but she knew she was the only one who could help them. They planned to go there a few days after the holidays.

Christmas was a great celebration. All of Eloise's family was together, enjoying a feast and giving gifts. Little Lui was so excited to celebrate Christmas with Eloise again. Everyone talked and laughed until the wee hours of the morning. Eloise felt happier than she had in a long time. It was so comforting to be home with family again.

A day later, Eloise told her parents that she needed to talk to them heart-to-heart. The three of them got together one evening after dinner. "I want to thank you," Eloise said, "for being so kind and supportive of my decisions. I want to let you know, Mom and Dad, that you mean the world to me."

"Eloise," her mother said, "we love you so much."

"No matter how far away I go," Eloise said, "you are there with me. I am so fortunate to have you as my parents. I'm sorry that I left you, but

I had to go to recover from losing Roger. I am better now, but I want to go back to the US to finish school and possibly to pursue a career in New York. I want your approval before I make this decision." Eloise's parents knew that she wanted to return to the United States.

"Whatever you choose to do with your life, we support you," her father said.

"Mom and Dad, I am not moving away from you. I am looking for a new horizon in my life."

"We know," her father said. "You should do whatever you think is best for you."

"We will come visit you in the US," her mother said. "We still want to bring Lui to Disney World." Eloise hugged her parents. She knew she could always count on them to support her.

Two days later, Eloise met with the Strausses for a final visit to Roger's apartment. They arrived early in the morning. Mr. Strauss opened the door and entered with his wife, Eloise following close behind. This was difficult for all of them. Eloise wanted to be strong, but she was the first one to start to sob. Tears came into her eyes so fast that she felt like she had to turn around and leave, but she stood firm. She knew she had to be strong for Mr. and Mrs. Strauss.

"Mrs. Strauss," Eloise said, "could we have someone else remove Roger's belongings? I don't think I can do it."

"Of course, dear," Mrs. Strauss said, tears coming into her own eyes. They had brought along the butler and the housekeeper, and Mrs. Strauss asked them to clean out the apartment.

"First, would you mind leaving me alone here for a few minutes?" Eloise asked. Everyone stepped outside, and Eloise knelt down on the floor. She closed her eyes and clasped her hands and began to pray to God. She prayed for Roger's soul, and then she asked God to help everyone heal, as the pain had been so unbearable. She promised God that she would go to church often to pray for Roger. Then she spoke to Roger, saying, "Roger, the love of my life, one day I may get married and have a family, but I will always hold your love in my heart. We will be together again one day. God be with you, my darling Roger. You were blessed, and that's why you died so young. God wants good people as part of his kingdom. You were chosen to be on his side, so please, my love, look out for us here on earth. Good-bye for now. I love you, my darling Roger." When Eloise left the apartment to meet the Strausses, they noticed that she looked different. It was as if she were glowing. Nothing needed to be said; they were finally ready for closure.

Then the day came for Eloise to return to the United States. It was sad to say good-bye to family and friends again, but when Eloise got back to school, she was occupied by her busy schedule. She contacted the company that had offered her a position as an interpreter in New York. They asked her to come in for another meeting to discuss the terms of the contract. Eloise brought her friend Lucia for another trip into the city. The company asked Eloise if she could come work for them in August. Eloise was thrilled and accepted the offer. She had just four months left of university, and then she would take some vacation time before moving to New York and starting her job.

CHAPTER FOURTEEN

The Strausses arrived in New York in early March to visit Eloise and their relatives. They enjoyed her company for a few days and then left for Vienna and Salzburg, where they would stay for the summer. While they were visiting, Eloise made plans to come see them in Europe over the summer.

After graduation, Eloise had six weeks before moving to New York and starting her new job. She went to visit the Strausses in Austria. They guided her around the countryside by car and train, showing her all the important sites in Austria and Switzerland.

When Eloise got back to the United States, she and Lucia found an apartment together. It was near the UN building and close to work for both of them. Eloise was very excited about her first job in the United States. The pay was great, and the people she would be working with were very well educated and knowledgeable. She was the Spanish and Portuguese interpreter in charge of the international company's Latin America division.

The job kept her on the move, and there was never a dull moment. One of the duties she most enjoyed was going to the airport to meet and greet dignitaries from all the countries her division represented. When she got home at night, she was exhausted but satisfied. Lucia worked for the same company, but she wasn't quite as busy as Eloise because she only interpreted Portuguese. They were both on call all the time, though, and often had to work on weekends. They always had the evenings free, though, and even left work in the early afternoon some days.

They decided to start an exercise routine. Lucia suggested joining a gym, but Eloise wanted to take a dance class. "Let's do ballet," she said. Lucia had never danced ballet, and this would be something totally new for her. She was skeptical, but Eloise urged her to try it. After the first few lessons, Lucia was hooked. Eloise loved being back in the dance studio.

Sometimes the girls would go out in the evenings, but they didn't have much time to date. As Brazilians, neither of them would ever dream of going to a bar or nightclub without a male escort. Once a week, they treated themselves to dinner at a nice restaurant. One evening, they felt particularly extravagant, so they dressed to the nines and went to a very expensive restaurant near their apartment.

When they entered, the maître d' said, "Ladies, you are both so beautiful. Are you movie stars from Hollywood?"

"Of course we are famous movie stars," Eloise said cockily, "but not from Hollywood—from Rio. Did you ever hear that song 'The Girl from Ipanema'?"

"Yes, I've heard it," the maître d' said, "but are there two girls?"

"Yes," Lucia said, playing along, "we are both the girls from Ipanema."

"Ladies," he said, "I will get you the best table, but I need to ask you both for an autograph later. Is it a deal?" Eloise and Lucia agreed.

They were seated across from a table of men who looked like executives. They appeared to be very involved in their business conversation until the girls sat down. They kept glancing over at Eloise and Lucia. When the waiter came over, he said the men had asked if they would accept a drink from them. "No, thank you," Eloise said.

The men weren't willing to give up that easily, though; they were very interested in meeting these two beauties. Eloise and Lucia continued to enjoy their dinner. At last one of the men dared to approach their table. "Hello," he said. "My name is Robert Clark. I don't wish to bother you, but you are the most beautiful ladies in this restaurant tonight. After your dinner, would you join me for a nightcap?"

"It's up to my friend," Lucia said. "We have other plans for the evening, though," she lied. Lucia hadn't noticed that during the meal Eloise had been exchanging flirtatious smiles with Robert.

"Yes, we'll have a drink with you after we finish our dinner," Eloise said.

After Robert walked away, Lucia leaned in close and raised her eyebrows at Eloise. "You little devil, you," she whispered. "Well, he is very handsome."

"Do you mind?" Eloise asked, a little embarrassed.

"It is fine by me, but we will go home together. I'm looking out for you. We don't know any of these guys."

"Of course," Eloise agreed. "We'll just have a chat with him, nothing else."

It was about ten o'clock when they finally finished their dinner. Robert approached the table again, and they asked him to sit down with them. Another man from Robert's table came by and asked if he could join them as well. He said his name was William Petersen. He was tall and handsome, with beautiful blue eyes.

They began to make small talk, and the men said they were attorneys and that they worked at the same firm along with the other men they had had dinner with. Both of them specialized in corporate law, had joined the firm around the same time, and were working toward becoming partners at the firm. They had been good friends for the past three years. Robert's family lived in Westchester County, about thirty minutes from New York City. William's family lived in Boston. They were in their early thirties and had gone to college in New York.

Eloise and Lucia talked with them for an hour, telling them a bit about themselves as well. At last Eloise and Lucia were ready to say good night to the gentlemen. When the waiter came by, Lucia asked him to call them a taxi. "Let us give you a ride home," Robert said, but Eloise and Lucia declined. The men gave them their business cards, but Lucia and Eloise didn't offer them their numbers. They had just met these two men, after all.

As time went by, the girls continued to be busy with work. When they had time off, they walked in Central Park and went to the occasional movie. They didn't have very active social lives because so much of their energy was invested in working.

In February, they decided to take a weekend off of work to go shopping. First, they went to Rockefeller Center to watch the ice skaters and eat breakfast. Later they would head to Fifth Avenue to window-shop. As they were sitting at the restaurant by the skating rink, Eloise felt a hand tap on her shoulder. She turned around and saw Robert smiling at her. "I cannot believe my eyes," he said. "It's Eloise and Lucia!"

"Robert!" Eloise said. "It's great to see you." It had been a month since they'd met at the restaurant.

"Where have you girls been?" he said. "I have been hoping I would run into you again. This is like magic." He asked them to have lunch or dinner with him that night.

"We're going shopping," Eloise said. "If I'm not too tired at the end of the day, I'll call you." Truthfully, Eloise was not sure if she wanted to go out with him alone. Robert handed her another business card, this time with his home phone number written on it.

After he walked away, Lucia said to Eloise, "If you want to go out with Robert, maybe it's okay. Just tell him that you will meet him at a restaurant. Go there by taxi and return home by taxi." Eloise was grateful to have such a good friend looking after her.

When Eloise called Robert, the first thing he asked was whether Lucia and William could both join them. Lucia was happy to hear this. She had secretly been wishing she would see William again. They made the date for Sunday.

Eloise and Lucia insisted on meeting Robert and William at the restaurant. It was probably the first time the men had been out with such cautious women. They had a wonderful night together. All four of them got along very well. At the end of the evening, they made plans to get together again the next week, during the day. They would take a walk in Central Park and then get lunch. Then Eloise and Lucia called a taxi to take them home. Robert and William knew better than to argue with them.

When Sunday rolled around, the girls said they would meet Robert and William at Tavern on the Green, a famous restaurant in Central Park, and then they would take a walk together. Eloise and Lucia still didn't want the men to know where they lived. Lucia was thrilled to be going out with Robert. "He's the most handsome guy I've ever dated," she told Eloise.

Four months passed, and both couples were getting closer. Robert invited Eloise to come meet his family in Westchester, and he asked Lucia and William to join them as well. Eloise was thrilled to finally meet Robert's family. He had two sisters who were married. One of them had three children, Robert's niece and two nephews. His other sister had been married for three years but didn't have any children yet. Robert's father was a medical doctor, and his mother was an interior decorator.

When they arrived, Robert brought Eloise and Lucia into the foyer and took their coats. Eloise could see that they had a lovely home. It was a co-lonial, decorated with fine antiques, family heirlooms, and a sophisticated art collection. Robert brought them to the family room, where his family was all together, waiting for their guests. He introduced Eloise and Lucia to his parents, sisters, niece, and nephews. Eloise noticed that Robert's parents and his sisters were all very good-looking. They gave Eloise and Lucia a warm welcome, making them feel at home right away.

When everyone sat down for dinner, the cook came out of the kitchen.

Eloise and Lucia were delighted to find out that she was from Brazil as well. They thought it was a hilarious coincidence. The cook's name was Claudia, and she had been working for the family for over twenty years. Robert's father met her on a trip to Brazil. He was there for a medical convention, and he met a Brazilian doctor. The two became friends, and Robert's father went back to visit for a month. During that time, he met Claudia and brought her back to the United States to work for him and his wife. They both loved Brazilian food. Claudia quickly adapted to her new life in the United States and decided to stay.

That evening was a special treat for Eloise and Lucia. They drank *caipirinhas*, the national drink of Brazil, made from liquor called *cachaça* mixed with sugar and lime. For dinner, they ate *feijoada*, a stew made of beans, beef, and pork. They finished the meal with a delicious traditional Brazilian dessert. It was an evening to remember.

"Can you believe it?" Lucia said to Eloise when they arrived home. "We almost didn't get to know those guys. They are the best."

Lucia was very taken by William. She was still getting to know him, but he had been a true gentleman in every way. Lucia and Eloise were both happy that they had boyfriends and could spend time together as a group. Lucia and Eloise worked together, lived together, and loved being best friends.

The summer was quickly approaching. Lucia and Eloise were not looking forward to the extreme heat of New York City, particularly Manhattan. When they had weekends off, they spent them in the Hamptons sailing, but most of the time they were busy with work.

Eloise still wanted to return to California. She told Lucia about her future plans. "I want to move by the end of the summer," she said.

"I don't want to interfere with your plans," Lucia said, "but I'm going to miss you. I am sad that I'll lose my best friend."

"You can come too," Eloise said. "Nothing is holding you back."

"What about William? We love each other," Lucia said. "I would miss him if I left, and I don't want to push my luck either. If I tell him I am going to California, it will sound like I'm giving him an ultimatum."

"I know you don't want to leave William," Eloise said.

"I'll come visit you," Lucia said.

"I really like Robert," Eloise said. "He's a wonderful man, but I'm not ready for a commitment. I can't stay here just because of him. I enjoy the work we're doing too, but there is no way I'm going to spend the rest of my life in the cold weather. I have friends in Palo Alto that I met when I was there before. We're still in touch, and they might be able to connect me with work there." Andrew was one of those friends. He had offered to help Eloise find an apartment and get a car.

On her next date with Robert, Eloise told him her plans. She could see the sadness and disappointment in his eyes. "If we got married, would you stay?" he asked.

"No, Robert," she said. "This isn't about you. Living in New York has been a great experience for me, but I don't want to deal with the snow and the cold weather."

"There is nothing I can say to convince you to stay?" Robert asked.

"No, I'm sorry. My mind is made up. I'm leaving in September," Eloise said. "Thank you for your love. It has been a great gift to know you. I do hope you'll come visit me in California."

The next two months were difficult for Eloise, Lucia, and Robert. She was leaving her closest friends, and she would miss them so much. Robert invited her to visit his family again before she left. Robert's whole family tried to talk her out of leaving, but like Robert had told them, her reasons were valid. "After all," Robert said, "she was born and raised in a warm climate. She is a tropical flower who needs the sun. I can understand that. I love the sunshine myself. Maybe I will move to California too."

His father interjected then. "Live your lives how and where you feel is the best for you, children. Life is short. You should never make yourselves unhappy to please others. Eloise, you may come back to New York and visit us anytime." Hearing this made Eloise happy. Up until then, she had been feeling guilty for walking away from her friends and all the wonderful people she had met in New York. Then other thoughts came to her mind. What about her own family? *Am I crazy?* she thought. *If I have to be anywhere, why not back home with them?* She started to think about going home to Brazil instead, but then she realized this was another step in her journey. She would proceed with her plans to go to California.

CHAPTER FIFTEEN

Eloise knew she had God on her side. She would often go to Mass or to pray at St. Patrick's Church. She loved that church. As she was sitting in the pews praying, looking up at the immense cross beneath colorful stained-glass windows, she would ask for God's protection and inspiration. Every time, she could feel Roger next to her, encouraging her to be brave and strong.

When the day came for Eloise to leave, Robert offered to take her to the airport, and Lucia went along. They exchanged many tearful hugs, and Robert and Lucia promised to visit.

The apartment that Andrew helped Eloise find was small but cute. It was in a huge apartment building with many amenities, including a pool, gym, tennis courts, and a lounge area for tenants to socialize. Eloise met a few people from the building right away. They all worked at companies in the area. Andrew also helped Eloise find a job. It was near Stanford University. She worked for an international company that needed someone fluent in Portuguese and Spanish. She was constantly in touch with her family in Brazil. They would call to check on her every week.

Life was good for Eloise. She made friends with a very nice woman from South America named Veronica. One night, Veronica asked her if she would like to go out to a nearby restaurant and nightclub with her and another friend, Maria.

When they arrived, the hostess showed them to their table. Eloise hadn't even sat down yet when a man approached her and asked her to dance. Eloise laughed. "Will you let me take off my coat first?" He was a nice-looking man.

"Yes," he said, helping her with her coat.

Veronica and Maria giggled, and then Veronica whispered in Eloise's ear, "He's so handsome. Go for it, friend."

"My name is Richard," the man said. Eloise could hear his British accent then. "May I have your name?"

"Eloise," she said.

"Your name is as pretty as you are," he said. "Forgive me for being so intrusive. I couldn't miss the chance to meet you, and I knew that if I waited, someone else would ask you to dance. I wanted to be the first." Eloise was very flattered. Richard was debonair and handsome. How lucky she was to meet him on her very first night out. Richard hung around Eloise the entire night, not leaving her alone for a moment. At the end of the evening, he offered to take her home.

"We're all going to go back together," Veronica said, since Eloise had just met Richard.

Eloise made plans with him to have lunch the next day, which was a Saturday. He came to pick her up in his Lexus convertible. Eloise, as always, looked beautiful. "Richard, do you mind putting the top up?" she asked. She didn't want her hair to get windblown and snarled; besides, it was cold out. Richard immediately complied and put up the convertible top.

They drove to a nearby restaurant for lunch. The chemistry between them was undeniable. They both enjoyed listening to each other's accents, his British and her Portuguese, as they laughed and talked all through lunch. At the end of the date, Richard dropped Eloise off at home and asked if he could see her again the next day. She agreed. Eloise truly enjoyed

Richard's company. He was sexy and charming and also considerate. He catered to Eloise's ever need or whim. Richard started to call Eloise every day, and soon they were inseparable. They met during their lunch breaks and then in the evening to see a movie or a show. They even took a trip to San Francisco.

After they had been seeing each other for a month, they went out one night. At the end of the evening, Richard dropped Eloise off and, as he always did, kissed her good night and then turned to leave. This time, Eloise did something different. She asked Richard to come up to her apartment for a cup of tea.

As they sat together on the living room couch, sipping their tea, Richard leaned in and kissed Eloise. She kissed him back passionately. They embraced and then took their affection to a more intimate level. Eloise asked Richard to stay with her that night. Richard was a gentleman and asked if he should use protection, but this time Eloise was prepared. She had been taking the pill.

Since it was their first night together, they were a bit shy in the beginning. Richard whispered romantic things to Eloise, and she felt more and more feminine and desired by him. She let go of her shyness, and they made love all night. It was spectacular.

In the morning, Richard stayed in bed with Eloise. When they got up, they showered together and then made love again. They didn't want to be apart, so they spent the whole day together. It was Sunday, and Eloise told Richard she wanted to go to church. To her surprise, he said he was also a Catholic. They went to the late Mass and then took a walk in the park. They both felt eager to share their lives with each other. Still, there was something sad in Richard's beautiful blue eyes that Eloise could not read. *Whatever it is, one day he will tell me,* she thought.

The weeks went by, and Veronica called Eloise to have lunch with her. As they ate, Veronica told Eloise that she knew someone who worked at the same firm with Richard. "Is he divorced yet?" Veronica asked.

"What?" Eloise said, "Divorced? Was he married?"

"Yes," Veronica said.

"He never told me that," Eloise said.

"Well, Eloise, for your information, he has two children," she said.

"You've got to be kidding, Veronica," Eloise said.

"No, I'm not. His wife is also British."

"He never mentioned any of this to me."

"Well, he might be waiting for the right moment," Veronica said. "If he doesn't bring it up, you should ask him. He was separated from his wife but went back to her, and then they separated again."

"I can't believe it," Eloise said, devastated.

"Sorry, but as your friend, I don't want to see you get hurt," Veronica said.

Eloise and Richard had planned to spend a weekend in Carmel. She was looking forward to it and decided not to spoil their plans. She would wait to ask Richard about what Veronica had told her. In Carmel, Eloise put her concerns aside, and they had the best weekend yet. On their last day there, they were having breakfast on the terrace of the cottage where they were staying. Eloise decided it was time to ask Richard. She looked him in the eyes and said, "Richard, why didn't you tell me about your personal life and your children?" Her tone of voice was kind and respectful but also demanded a response. "Are you still married?" she said. "How is your relationship with your wife now?"

Richard couldn't believe what he was hearing, but he was also relieved that Eloise knew his secret. "Eloise," he said, "I didn't want to lose you. There were many times when I wanted to tell you, but each time I hesitated because I was afraid you wouldn't want to see me again. We're not divorced yet, but we have agreed to get divorced. I was only twenty-three when I got married, and my children are very young. It breaks my heart, but their mother and I fight all the time, and it's not good for them."

"I understand," Eloise said, "but I can't date a married man. What if you decide to reconcile with your wife for the sake of the kids? Then where will I be?"

"Eloise, please," Richard begged, "I am in love with you. It was hard for me not to tell you, but I wasn't brave enough to do it."

"I have no intention of being someone's mistress," Eloise said. "We have to stop seeing each other right now so that you are free to make your own decision. I'm not asking you to choose. You just need time to think without me getting in the middle of it."

Richard took her hand and said, "Please, my love, do not leave me now. I need you in my life."

"I want you in my life too," Eloise said, "but what I don't need is pain and heartbreak. Let's take time out. If you decide to go back to your family, I will understand. I lost the man I love to death; nothing can be worse than that."

"Eloise, I love you," Richard said.

"I love you too," Eloise said, "but if we are to be together, you have to make a final decision. You can take my love with you. I have not felt this connection with anyone since my fiancé died." Tears sprang into Richard's eyes as Eloise spoke.

"Then, until my divorce is final, be with me not as a lover but as a friend."

"Okay," Eloise said. "We'll still see each other as friends."

CHAPTER SIXTEEN

When Eloise was back in Palo Alto, she received an offer for a job in San Francisco at an international travel agency. She'd have to give it thought. She would like to be in San Francisco—she was a city girl after all. She told Richard about the job, and he said he thought it would be a great opportunity for her. Although he lived and worked in Palo Alto, he often thought about moving to San Francisco.

As Eloise was considering the offer, she received another offer from a company that was also based in San Francisco. This job was at the biggest bank in the United States. She consulted with Richard again. "My dear Eloise," he said, "the travel agency is the right choice for you. Remember, your family lives far away. If you work for the travel agency, you'll have the chance to travel back and forth to visit them. Besides, with your language skills, it will be a great working environment for you."

"That's true," Eloise said.

"Before you make a final decision, be sure to ask questions of both companies." Eloise did as Richard suggested and decided to take the job with the travel agency. She realized that she would have been bored working for a bank.

Just a few weeks later, Eloise was moving to San Francisco. She got an apartment in the Marina district, which was near everything. She settled in and felt happy. It wasn't long before she heard from Richard. He said that as soon as he was able, he too would be moving to San Francisco.

Eloise made many friends in her new job. There were at least eighty people working in the office, and they seemed to come from every corner of the world. She could get help from her coworkers with almost any language. Eloise had found exactly what she needed right now—a new city, new friends, and a new career. It was exciting.

Eloise immediately became close with the woman who was training her. She was a charming and delightful woman from Bern, Switzerland. Her name was Liselot, but she went by the nickname Lilo. Many people wanted to call Eloise Lilo too, because their names sounded so similar. Eloise didn't like that, though, and would always correct people, saying, "Please call me Eloise. That is my name, thank you." Lilo introduced Eloise to a group of friends in the neighborhood who worked for airlines. The major carriers had offices in Union Square in downtown San Francisco. They all gathered together to walk to Chinatown for lunch every Friday. One of Eloise's new friends invited her to take a free trip to Disneyland. Later she got to go to Hawaii too. Eloise was really happy with her new job.

Richard was in touch often. He was going ahead with his divorce. When they talked, he sounded both happy and sad. He was glad to be leaving his marriage but unhappy about being separated from his children. Still, he knew he had to move on with his life.

After Eloise moved to San Francisco, her father told her to look up the Brazilian consulate. He had an old friend named Alvarez Dias who moved to California some years ago and worked for the consulate. Eloise's father thought that perhaps she could connect with him. "If you find him, tell him that I want to ask him to look after my little girl," he said. Eloise first contacted the consulate in Los Angeles. They knew Mr. Dias and said that he had acted as a temporary replacement for a consulate some years back when Carmen Miranda was in Hollywood. Since then, he had moved to

San Francisco. Eloise managed to track him down. He and his wife, Talia, came to meet Eloise at her office. They went out for lunch together, and Eloise enchanted the older couple.

Eloise was grateful to have found them. She missed having a mother and father figure in her life, since she was away from her parents. Alvarez and Talia called Eloise often to invite her for dinner at their house; to introduce her to their friends; and to take her to concerts, operas, and plays. They had a beautiful home atop the hills in San Francisco with a fantastic view of the Golden Gate Bridge.

Eloise's parents were pleased that Eloise had become such close friends with the Diases. The Christmas holidays were drawing near, and Eloise could not take time off from work to go to see her family, so Alvarez and Talia invited Eloise to spend Christmas with them. They had a son, daughter, and grandchildren who would be coming to spend the holidays with them too, so Eloise would not be alone.

Eloise was still seeing Richard on a regular basis. He had finally moved to San Francisco from Palo Alto, but he was a little vague as to when his divorce would be final. Eloise introduced him to her new friends, the Diases. They liked Richard very much, and the feeling was mutual. Eloise was so happy with her new job that her love life was not her priority.

She had a good social life, and she spent a lot of time taking ballet lessons. She found a beautiful Catholic church to attend near her apartment in Pacific Heights. She would go there often to pray and sometimes for Sunday Mass. For some reason, Roger had been very much in her thoughts lately. *Maybe he is up there somewhere, thinking of me too*, she thought. She would often wake up thinking of the man she loved more than any other. He had inspired her to be the best she could be and would forever remain in her prayers.

Eloise was very sad about not being able to see her family on Christmas. They made lots of phone calls and sent loving cards to each other. Eloise wanted her parents to feel confident that she was happy. The days and weeks went by, and soon the beautiful celebrations of Christmas arrived. Eloise and Richard were invited to spend a night with the Diases to celebrate New Year's Eve. They all had a wonderful time together, waiting for midnight to begin the new year all together. When the clock struck midnight, they all cheered and gave one another hugs and kisses.

Eloise continued to write letters home. In one letter, she told her parents how much she loved the United States and its people. "They are great people," she wrote. "They are very discrete, hardworking, and have a *live and let live* attitude, which I love." She had only good things to say about her new friends and her adopted country. She wanted her parents to visit her and get to know this beautiful country. Her mother, who didn't like to travel by plane, said maybe one day she would gather the courage to fly again. The spring came, and soon Eloise would be taking a trip to Brazil to see her family.

Richard was being a little evasive about their relationship—not calling her and not answering her calls. One day she decided to stop by his apartment to say hello. When she walked in the door, he was there with a girl. She was very young looking, probably a teenager. Eloise felt awkward, and so did Richard. She apologized for the intrusion and left. At that point, she had had it with Richard. She did not need that type of person in her life. He could have at least ended their relationship before going off with another woman, a child no less. From that day on, she erased him from her mind. He called a few times, but she didn't return his calls.

Eloise took her trip to Brazil. It was pure joy to see her family again. She stayed for a whole month. When Eloise got back to work, her friend Lilo invited her to come to Switzerland in the fall. Lilo was going back to her country to get married. When the fall came, Eloise went to Switzerland. Lilo's family embraced Eloise right away, making her feel welcome. She stayed in Bern with Lilo, but they traveled to all the major cities. Geneva was her favorite city in Switzerland. Lilo's wedding was going to be later in the year, so Eloise would not be there for it; however, she enjoyed her trip so much she knew she would be back to Switzerland again. When she returned to work, she missed her dear friend. She was not dating anyone, so her social life was focused on friends and going to concerts, operas, and museums.

Richard continued to pursue Eloise. She did not want to see him again but eventually gave in. They started to spend some time together. Eloise was sure she didn't want to be intimately involved with Richard, but it was difficult because they had such powerful chemistry together. What she felt when she was near Richard was unlike anything Eloise had ever experienced before. She was drawn to him like a magnet.

She wanted to focus on having a platonic relationship with him; after all, they had a lot in common, they both had lovely personalities and a similar level of education, and they enjoyed each other's company. They could have been friends forever, but when they were together, the fire of their desire was impossible to control. They invariably ended up in bed together. It scared Eloise because she knew that Richard was a terrible womanizer, and she could not put up with that.

Two years had passed since they first met. Richard asked Eloise to go out with him; he said he had news to share about his life and career. Richard was a good friend above all, so she said yes. They went out for dinner, and after the waiter had brought them each a glass of wine, Richard made his announcement. "I got an offer from a major international company. The job is in England." Eloise was sad to lose him, but she shared his enthusiasm.

"Congratulations, Richard!" she said, raising her glass for a toast.

They clinked glasses, and then Richard said, "If I accept the position, I'll be leaving California in a month."

"What about your kids?" Eloise asked. His children were still young—just two and four years old. Eloise wondered what Richard's ex-wife would do without him nearby to support.

"They'll be okay," Richard said, and then he left it at that. Eloise had been disappointed in Richard when she discovered she was cheating on him, but now she felt something much worse. She was losing respect for him. On the other hand, she reasoned that Richard was young and had the right to pursue his career. She decided not to think about the matter any further. After all, each person chooses his or her own destiny. Eloise secretly knew that this was the end of their relationship. She had to move on.

She planned a vacation that coincided with Richard's departure. She would go back to Brazil to see her family. She asked for two weeks of vacation and two weeks of unpaid leave so that she could be with them for a full month.

CHAPTER SEVENTEEN

When Eloise arrived home, her family's welcome warmed her heart. She loved to visit with her parents, brother, and sisters. She spent a lot of time reliving all her wonderful memories of Roger and her life with him. His parents were still in Austria; they had decided to stay there for a few years. After Roger died, it was very difficult for them to be in Brazil, although Eloise knew that eventually they would return. Eloise ended up staying in Brazil for three months.

She returned to the United States with the resolve to further her career, and when she arrived, she was offered a position with a major airline. Eloise accepted the position, and a new life started to take shape—she made new friends, and there were lots of perks at her new job.

Eloise became good friends with a woman named Nancy who was a lawyer. Eloise wanted her own apartment, but since Nancy was such a good friend, they decided to look for an apartment together. They were both Catholics, had similar backgrounds, came from good families, and were both very busy in their careers. Nancy was engaged to an attorney who was a great support to both of them.

Richard got in touch with Eloise and asked her to visit him in London. She resisted for a while but finally decided, *Why not?* She thought to herself,

We will be lovers again, and that is what I need. Eloise was a vey sensuous and sexy woman but also very conservative. It would take a man a lot of time to prove that he was worthy of her. Never had she gone to bed with a man on the first date. She was fussy and choosey. Since breaking up with Richard, there had not been another man in her life. They had not seen each other for a year now, and she wanted to.

Eloise packed her bags and went to London. Richard looked as charming and gorgeous as ever. She only had two weeks to spend with him, and she wanted to see London and enjoy her time off. It was a great vacation for her, and at the end of the trip, she accompanied Richard to Bermuda for a few days before returning to the United States. When she got back, she was refreshed, and it felt great to get back to work.

Five months had passed since Eloise's visit with Richard when she received a letter from him announcing his engagement to a woman he was dating. Eloise read the letter several times before it sank in. *I cannot believe my eyes,* she thought. *How dare he?*

The next night, when Eloise got home, Nancy told her that she had received some red roses. They were delivered with a card. Eloise opened the card. The roses were from Richard. On the same day, she also received a letter from Richard. Richard wrote, "I am engaged to a wonderful girl. She is nineteen and beautiful. I am happy with her, and I think you would be pleasantly surprised if you met her. Our wedding will be in May."

Eloise didn't know how to react. Nancy was honest. "Eloise, this is a great thing. Now you have to realize that you must go on with your life. You have to get this man out of your life forever."

"Yes," Eloise said. "You are right about that, but can he take me out of his life? We will see. This marriage is too premature, but that is Richard— the rascal. I am sure our paths will cross again one day."

Eloise met a nice man through a friend she knew from another airline. His name was John, and he was very keen on Eloise, but Eloise did not feel the same. John had dated a Brazilian girl in college for a while, but the long distance didn't help, and the relationship ended. He was still very fond of the Brazilian people and wanted Eloise to go out with him. Eloise accepted his invitation, and soon they were going out once a week.

John invited Eloise to his parents' house for a barbecue. It was a pleasant Sunday with John's family, and Eloise got to know his parents, brothers, and sister. His family was very religious. They didn't drink any alcohol or even coffee, and they believed that sex should only come after marriage.

Eloise did not know much about John's religion and did not dwell on it. It didn't seem important to her because they were just friends. In a way, she felt safe because she knew he was not going to try to seduce her. John took Eloise to Lake Tahoe for skiing, which she loved. He always had a very respectful attitude, and they slept in separate bedrooms.

They continued to date, and Eloise was enjoying life. Her social life was exciting and fun, and she liked her work and the camaraderie among her coworkers. As time went on, John asked Eloise if she would marry him. She said, "I have to think about that. I need to get to know you better."

When Eloise got home, she told Nancy that John had asked her to marry him. "My goodness," Nancy said. "Eloise, what was your response to that?"

"I told John we have to get to know each other better."

"Eloise, you have to get to know him more intimately. Marriage is a serious step. I have been dating Tom for over a year. I love him, and I know he loves me too. Like you, I need to get to know him a little longer before we get married. We have to find out more about how we get along on other matters, like dealing with money for instance, having a family, and so on. You have to get to know John better and see how it will work for both of you." Nancy's advice was wise; Eloise knew she had to give it time.

Eloise's office was a fun place to be. There were three hundred plus employees from all walks of life and cultures. It was a melting pot. About ten or more languages were spoken, and there was always some excitement going on.

Eloise and her coworkers were reservation agents for the airlines. They were in contact with the public on a daily basis and always had interesting stories about the questions they were asked. One day, a friend told Eloise about a woman who called. She didn't speak English very well and kept saying, "What time does the plane crash at the San Jose airport?" The woman meant to ask, "What time does the plane land?" Another agent was asked whether he was a person or a robot. He answered, "Yes, ma'am, I am a robot." The midnight crew had even more bazaar stories. Eloise and her friends always had something to laugh about at the office.

Once an acquaintance said to Eloise, "You are so well educated and sophisticated. Why do you work for an airline? You could be making a lot more money as an executive for an international company."

"You might be right," Eloise said, "but I have chosen a career that I enjoy. Money and prestige come at a price that I am not willing to pay. I could have gone to work in Washington, DC, or stayed in New York for my career, but I am not a career woman. I work to pay my bills, but I want to enjoy life. I feel good about myself. I chose the place that I want to live and the people I want in my life. I need my freedom. I love to travel, to get to know places and explore the world. There is so much to see. I also want to have a family one day, and a job that demands too much from me would not fit into my lifestyle. I have been around career women. I am not made for that kind of life; I am made for love. I have a purpose in this world, and every day, when I wake up, I thank God for my life. I don't demand much. I am grateful for what I am given—good health and time to appreciate it. Life is too short. If I am to be wealthy, it will come to me, but I am rich from being a good lamb of God." Eloise had many opportunities to travel and meet great people. Now she was ready for the next best thing, which she thought might be getting more serious about a relationship.

CHAPTER EIGHTEEN

Eloise was still dating John, and she admired him for his devotion and love for her. He was so patient with her, never demanding anything. He was just there at all times. One night, they went out for dinner, and Eloise told him that they should talk more seriously about his marriage proposal. "We have to get to know each other more intimately and discuss what it would be like if we got married," Eloise said.

John agreed. "Would you go away with me for a weekend, so we can talk about it?" he asked. Eloise agreed, and they took their first three-day weekend away together. It was a nice mellow weekend. There was no excitement, but John was sweet. He told Eloise he would be a devoted husband, caring for her every need. He also told her that he wanted a family. Eloise was very clear on the subject. She would have one or maybe two children. She came from a large family, and she knew she didn't want more than two children. Their first night together was not a passionate one but adequate enough to seal their relationship. They came back from that weekend officially engaged.

Eloise called her family to announce the engagement and tell her parents about the man she was going to marry. They asked Eloise to please come to Brazil for the wedding. She asked John, and he agreed. Eloise realized that for them to be married in a Catholic church, John would have to be christened as a Catholic. She would have to discuss it with him. She hoped it wouldn't be a problem. John's family was delighted about the engagement, especially John's father, who showed great affection for this future daughter-in-law.

John was so in love with Eloise that he told her he was beside himself with happiness over having met her. They decided to get married in a few months, giving time for wedding preparations. In the meantime, Eloise and John were together as much as they could be, but they had different working schedules, which interfered with their time together. Eloise and John occasionally spent a weekend together, discussing their future. Eloise was cautious and made sure to protect herself from getting pregnant before the wedding.

One day, she discovered that her period was late. She didn't panic but decided to call her doctor. When the date of her appointment finally came around, she was three weeks late. The pregnancy test came back positive. Eloise was not prepared for this. She called John and asked him to have dinner with her at her apartment. He came over, and they had a pleasant evening together. After dinner, Eloise told him that she was pregnant. "Well," John said, "let's get married now then."

"I promised my parents we'd get married in Brazil," Eloise said.

"We can have a civil ceremony here and then get married in a church in Brazil." The decision was made. They took a plane to Las Vegas and eloped. When their friends heard, they were disappointed. They had wanted to go to the wedding. Eloise and John found a place to move in together and eventually had a small party for their closest friends. At that same party, they announced that they were expecting a baby. Eloise's family was so happy that she had a good husband and would realize her dream to have a baby.

Eloise chose not to find out what sex the baby was. At her baby shower, the baby things came in all colors. Eloise's pregnancy was far from easy.

She was so tiny, weighing only ninety-seven pounds. Her doctor was concerned about her eating well and resting, but Eloise wanted to work until she was at least eight months pregnant and then take at least six months of maternity leave after her baby was born.

John was a very nice man, but he was also introverted and insecure. Eloise had not seen this aspect of his character before they were married, and it made it difficult to communicate with him. To make up for it, he was attentive and kind in many ways. Eloise and John's married life was without excitement and also without problems.

Eloise had finally figured out that John was Mormon. She didn't know much about Mormons except that they were clean cut, did not drink alcohol or caffeine, and didn't smoke. Eloise admired their discipline, but she didn't know it would be a test of their marriage later on. If a Mormon marries someone outside the religion, his or her spouse is expected to convert, especially if it is the wife. John's sister married a Catholic, who soon converted to Mormonism.

John's family started to plead with Eloise, saying, "You must convert." Even when they weren't mentioning it outright, they hinted at it. Eloise ignored them completely. She would often go to church on Sundays. At first John tried to go to church with her, but his religion was so different he couldn't relate to the Catholic Masses. Eloise had to accept this, because neither one of them had any intention to convert to the other's religion. Eloise had told John from the beginning that their child would be christened as a Catholic and would go to a Catholic school, and he agreed. John told her that he had been more involved with his church before he married her.

"I will respect your choices if you respect mine," Eloise said.

Eloise was a divine human being. She had deep faith and inner confidence, so much so that it was hard for others to understand. Religion, love, and faith in good were incredibly important to her. She always walked tall; she never hated or looked back with regret. Her motto was that there was nothing they couldn't handle. With her incredible inner strength, she moved mountains on her way up.

Despite her vast intelligence, Eloise was humble and respectful. She never behaved arrogantly toward others. She was always willing to listen to advice from others; she took it all in and then selected the advice that suited her best. Eloise was still very pretty and fashion conscious. Her friends often asked her to help them shop for clothes or choose makeup. Even though she was only 5'2," when Eloise walked into a room, all eyes were on her. Men flocked to her, admiring her beauty. Women would sneer at her with jealousy, but Eloise was always poised and kind to everyone.

Pregnancy was hard on Eloise, but John was caring and attentive. She also had support from other women in her office. There were five of them in the office who were all expecting within four months of each other. Eloise found it comforting to have other women in the same situation whom she could talk to. Her supervisor joked with them, saying, "Did you conspire this baby thing? I can't believe it—five babies! That's a first. I hope you'll all continue to work." There were baby showers galore—one after the other.

Pregnancy became even more difficult for Eloise after her fifth month. Her doctor, Dr. Reimer, was concerned that she was not eating well or taking her vitamins. She had become afraid to eat too much, because she didn't want to get fat. Her doctor made her promise she would eat, regardless of the weight gain. She was so tiny that she didn't start to show until her sixth month.

Eloise started to think how life would change once she had the baby. Just a few months earlier, she had been one of the stars of travel in the office. She was always on a plane somewhere—London, Paris, New York, and the list goes on. She would go for shopping trips for a few days or fly to Rio to see her family. In a way, she was ready to settle down with a new baby to fill her life.

When she was eight and half months pregnant, Eloise was invited to a reception honoring a Brazilian celebrity who was visiting San Francisco. She wanted to go so badly, but John was worried about her going out to a big party at night. He tried to talk her out of it, but Eloise was determined to go. John went with her, and they had a great time with friends and other guests. When they arrived home, Eloise was exhausted but happy. She had almost stolen the show because she was the only pregnant woman in the room. The celebrity himself came to wish her the best with her new baby and told her in a whisper, "I hope you have a girl—they are the best. I have three girls and one boy. My wife would not give up until we had a boy, but I experienced the joy of my three girls for six years." Hearing this made Eloise wonder if they would have a girl. She didn't really care, though. She prayed that God would send them a healthy baby—boy or girl.

In August, Eloise had a baby girl. She named her Marie Christine. She was six and half pounds and as beautiful as an angel. She had blue eyes, rosy cheeks, and ten fingers and toes. She was healthy and wonderful, which was exactly how the pediatrician described her. Eloise's life was going to change forever. Eloise's little princess would take her mom's life by storm. Eloise started trying to nurse on the second day of her baby's life. It was awkward and frustrating at first because, like most babies, Christine didn't know how to nurse right away. Eloise was worried that her baby was hungry and unable to eat. She said to the nurse, "Maybe we should give her a bottle."

"No," the nurse said, "you have to be patient and keep trying." Eloise did, and eventually little Christine started nursing. After that, all she wanted to do was eat and sleep. She was a joy, and Eloise found herself praying to God every day, thanking him for giving her this beautiful little angel. At two months, Christine was christened. Despite the pressure from John's family to convert to Mormonism, Eloise was firm in her beliefs. "Neither Christine nor I will ever convert—end of conversation," she said to John.

Something shifted in their relationship after that, and they become less and less communicative and colder toward one another. When Eloise would visit John's family, she sometimes heard them making fun of other races and religions. One night, at the end of a long, boring dinner conversation, John started participating in the jokes about Catholics. Eloise had enough of their insults and bad manners. She excused herself from the room, picked up her little baby who was asleep in a bedroom, got the car keys that John had left near the baby's crib, and snuck out of the house unnoticed. She drove back home alone. It was after 9:00 p.m., and Eloise was a little scared at first, but she kept driving until she got home, more than thirty miles away. She had left her husband without a word.

At home, Eloise brought her baby to bed with her and went to sleep. The next day, John came home looking puzzled and angry. She realized he was not the person she thought he was. He didn't ask why she left alone; he knew why but was afraid to bring it up. She decided she didn't care and didn't bother to explain herself.

John suggested they sleep in separate rooms, and Eloise agreed. She moved Christine's crib to her bedroom, and John and Eloise lived separate lives from then on. Eloise would not leave John because she felt it was important that Christine have two parents to support her.

CHAPTER NINETEEN

Time went by, and soon Christine was thirteen. The family had moved to the suburbs because Eloise did not want her child to live a city life. Eloise was a devoted mother, and Christine was a delightful girl—singing and laughing all the time. She became a great skier and swimmer and a child model.

Christine was strikingly beautiful, and the photographers loved to take pictures of her. She had beautiful blue eyes and gorgeous dark brown hair, a chiseled face with high cheek bones, and luminous skin. At thirteen, Christine was not into boys. This was a relief for Eloise, who wanted Christine to stay innocent and not to think about boys at such a young age.

Eloise had many hobbies of her own—she was still dancing ballet, and her newest interest was ballroom dancing. At Christmastime, she received a card from Richard's stepmother. He was still living in Europe with his wife, but his stepmother said he was anxious to hear from Eloise. She sent Eloise his address and asked her to contact him.

Of all the men she had known, Richard was her favorite after Roger. He was charming, polite, a true gentleman—and a rascal and womanizer nevertheless. Despite his flaws, she enjoyed his company, and, after her beloved Roger, he had been the best love she ever had. She sent Richard a card and immediately received a response. He invited Eloise and her family to visit him and his family in Europe. She talked to her husband about it, and they decided to take a little vacation to visit Richard.

Richard's wife was pretty and much younger than Richard. They had an adorable daughter whom Christine had a good time playing with. The trip was only a week long, but it reaffirmed Eloise's suspicion that Richard was still attracted to her. She felt good about that. For the past seven years, she had had absolutely no sexual contact with her husband. She wanted to be loved again; after all, she was still so young and pretty.

When they returned home, Eloise enrolled in a ballroom dancing class with a very famous teacher, Roberto Dantez. He owned the dance school, and lessons with him were expensive, but she wanted the best teacher. She started taking three lessons a week and loved every minute of it. Roberto was a genius at his craft. "My God," Eloise would say. "When I am dancing with him, I don't care if the world stops." Her favorite dance turned out to be the Viennese waltz. It brought back memoires of her days dancing with Roger. Roberto was tall, handsome, and single, but Eloise knew what a famous, good-looking man like Roberto could do to a woman's heart. In addition to being a dance teacher, he was a choreographer, an entrepreneur, and a very accomplished actor.

Roberto asked Eloise to be his partner in a show he was dancing in. "Oh my God, Roberto, I cannot dance in front of a group of people," she said. "I would be terrified."

"My dear Eloise," he said, "if that is the reason you won't do it, I guess you will agree to rehearse with me for a couple of weeks before the show." They started dancing five days a week. She performed like a professional. He was delighted at how quickly Eloise picked up the steps and was so gracious on the floor. The show was a success. They got a standing ovation. Roberto was a gentleman on the dance floor, and he stood back and motioned for the applause to go to Eloise. She was in tears when they got behind the curtain. Roberto embraced her and thanked her. Then Roberto asked Eloise to go out for dinner with him. He had a girlfriend, but that night they would celebrate their success, just the two of them. Eloise accepted Roberto's invitation. She needed to be around positive people like Roberto. He was her dance teacher, but over the last few months, he had also been a very special companion to her.

Roberto was always joking, laughing, and having a great time. She enjoyed the dinner so much. That night she went home to her beautiful daughter but also to her boring and meaningless marriage. Sometimes Eloise considered divorce, but she wanted to wait until her daughter was older. Roberto called Eloise the next day and asked her to go with him to see a show in the city that day. They would be gone for the day.

She said, "Yes," happy for an excuse to escape from John. She wanted to bring Christine, but she had plans to go on a picnic with her best friend and her family.

Eloise and Roberto went to see a country-dance show. It was a first for Eloise, and she learned a few more dance steps that day. It was dusk when the show ended, and they stopped at a nice little restaurant before heading home. Roberto looked so handsome. His shirt was a little open, showing off his beautiful physique. He had a great smile too. Eloise could hardly hide her attraction to him. Roberto confessed that he wished to spend more time with Eloise. When they got back to his car, he couldn't stop himself from grabbing Eloise and kissing her passionately. She was a sensual woman and kissed him back. She didn't care about anything else in that moment. "I am afraid of falling in love with you," she confessed to Robert. "You have a steady relationship with your girlfriend, Natalie."

"You're married," he said. "What do you want to do?" he asked.

"I want to spend time with you," Eloise responded. "There will be consequences to deal with, but I want to fall in love again. I want to feel wanted and loved." They planned a weekend together. Eloise was so elated at the prospect of being with Roberto that she was counting the days until their trip. She had to find a way to keep the trip a secret. Christine spent a lot of time with her best friend, Amy, and often asked if she could spend a weekend with her. Eloise told Christine to plan the weekend with Amy; meanwhile she would go away with Roberto that same weekend. Roberto made all the arrangements.

When the weekend came, they went to Lake Tahoe, where Roberto had a cabin in the mountains. It was late fall, but there was no snow on the ground yet. The cabin had a huge fireplace and a spectacular view from the balcony. Eloise could hardly believe how beautiful and awesome it was. Their first night there, Roberto was very respectful. He showed Eloise that the cabin that had two bedrooms and two bathrooms. Eloise, not wanting to be forward, dropped her bag in the guest room. They bought groceries and prepared a nice dinner together. He didn't drink alcohol, but he bought champagne and wine for Eloise. After dinner, they sat next to the fireplace and kissed again. This time the chemistry between them was amazing. Roberto took Eloise to the master bedroom, where they made passionate love. For Eloise, it was the pinnacle of her sexual experience. They spent the next two days in total ecstasy.

Eloise got up in the morning to make coffee for them, and Roberto followed her to the kitchen. He raised his mug of coffee and confessed that he was in love with her and he had been for sometime. "Me too," Eloise replied.

"Let us just be happy, my love," he said. "Let destiny lead our way. If we must be only lovers, let us be. I want more than that, though; I want you to be my wife. I am not going to force any responsibilities on you now, though. I will wait for you for as long as it takes." This was the love that Eloise needed, and she would not let anything or anyone interfere.

They stayed together for three nights. When she returned home, Christine was still with her friend. John did not even ask where she had been. She and Roberto were a great couple. They were beautiful, graceful dancers and very popular around town. Eloise didn't care what her reputation might be. She was married yet having a torrid love affair with her dance teacher. She didn't stop to think of the consequences.

Roberto asked Eloise to marry him, but she didn't even want to think about taking such a huge step, not now. This was a time in her life when she needed love and laughter, but marrying Roberto was not in her plans. She tried to explain this to him without hurting his feelings, but he was in love with her and terribly worried that she would reject him. He asked her if she would leave her husband for him. Eloise was confused by the question. "Roberto, I love being with you," she said. "You have done so much for me. You taught me ballroom dancing, and our personal relationship has taken me to a new level in my life, but I need to spend time with my daughter. I do not want to cause trauma to her."

"Eloise," Roberto said, "your daughter might be upset at first, but she will understand."

"With all due respect for you, you are my lover and friend and so much more, but she is my priority," Eloise said. "I have given up a lot for her, and that is not going to change now. One day it might, but I have to see her through college and get her started on her career path before I can find myself again."

"Eloise, please," Roberto begged, "you have to think of your own happiness too."

"My daughter didn't ask to be born. I gave her life, and I am responsible for her," she said. "I am sorry if you cannot understand my point of view. I would like to continue to dance with you and to be your lover, but that is all I can offer you now."

"I understand," Roberto said glumly. "I am not happy, but I understand. I was the same way. I was very young when I married my girlfriend, who was pregnant. I was eighteen, and she was sixteen. I know how it is to have responsibilities."

Eloise and Roberto continued to dance and spend time together as much as they could. They decided not to let anything interfere with their great love affair. Eloise found herself at a crossroads. She hated to carry on an extramarital affair; however, it was very hard to break up with Roberto. In a way, she was in love with the great times she was having with him. Time would determine whether they had a future together. Whatever happened, Eloise knew in her heart that she would always cherish their time together. If nothing else, she wanted to continue to have Roberto in her life as a friend and a teacher. She knew that he was in love with her and felt guilty for encouraging that to happen. They continued seeing each other despite the conflict the relationship caused in her life.

Meanwhile, John was trying to get closer to Eloise. He had even tried to force her to be intimate with him, which was something that had never happened before. One day John brought her flowers and asked her to go out for the night on a date with him. *Of course*, she thought; after all, they were married. "Let's go out and have a nice night out together." To Eloise's dismay, it was the most boring evening. There was no affection between them, and the conversation was impersonal. All John talked about was business and money, nothing else. When they returned home, he said, "Good night," and went straight to his bedroom.

As Eloise lay in her own bed, she thought for a long time before falling asleep. *My God, what happened to my life?* she thought. *Here I am, married to someone I can hardly communicate with. Yes, I am married to the father of my darling daughter, and he loves and cares for her. With both of her parents together, she is protected and sheltered and well taken care of financially. But what kind of a marriage is this? I married a man who does not talk to me. He is aloof, cold, and totally disconnected from everything around him. At least Roberto took me out of my misery and brought excitement into my life again.* Eloise remembered that some years ago a friend referred to her as a happy girl. Eloise knew who she was, and she had her cross to bear. She was a true believer; she knew that one day the light would shine brightly in her life. She was grateful for her daughter, Christine, her bright little star who always gave her the love she needed. She had many friends and an adoring family who loved her too.

Eloise had heard from Richard again. He was going to visit the Unites States to see some relatives and friends in California. He would come see Eloise and her family too, and he asked if he could stay with them for a few days. Eloise agreed; Richard and his wife had been very good hosts to her family when they went to Europe.

When Richard and his wife came, it was a pleasant visit but a little awkward. She and Richard had incredible chemistry that would not fade. As soon as they were alone together, Eloise said, "Richard, please stop flirting with me in front of your wife and my husband!"

"I can't help it, Eloise," he said. "You are so sexy and desirable."

"My God, Richard," Eloise said, "you are so naughty."

"I wish my wife and your husband were the ones who were together. They are alike—cold and dull. I made a big mistake, Eloise. I should have ended up with you."

"Richard, stop," Eloise said. "What are you proposing, to run away? To have an affair?"

"I don't know," Richard said. "Maybe."

"No, Richard, this is unfair," she said. "We are married to other people, and we have children. We have responsibilities to our spouses, and think of the consequences." Richard crossed his arms and shook his head, clearly disappointed. "I loved you once, and you left me for someone else. Now you want me back in your life?" Eloise continued. "On what conditions? It's just not right."

"Fine, Eloise," Richard said. "I'll leave you alone."

"Just give me some time to think," Eloise said. She could see that Richard was frustrated and unhappy. She wasn't happy either, but she knew she could never be with Richard. In hindsight, she wondered how she could have longed for Richard when Roger had always been her true love. Roger had been so kind, a true gentleman, and the desire they had for each other was like a roaring fire.

Eloise couldn't begin to imagine taking a whole new direction in her life. She continued on, stuck in the same routine. After Richard and his wife left, Eloise didn't see him for two years. They kept in touch, though. Christine graduated from high school and decided to stay close to home, which pleased Eloise. Christine enrolled in a two-year college and would decide later where she would continue her studies.

Richard came back into Eloise's life. Now he had divorced his wife, but he was dating an Italian girl whom he had met while he was still married. That was Richard—he could never be alone. Richard called Eloise a few times to chat. That Italian love affair did not last. When they finally met up again, Eloise joked with him about the failed affair. "You see, Richard," she said, "you are wasting your time. You keep looking for me in every woman you meet. Give it up. I've been the woman you've been searching for since day one."

"If that's true, why didn't I just hold onto you when I had you?" Richard asked.

"I scared you because I represented everything you always wanted," Eloise said. "But never mind, my darling, maybe we should carry on with our love affair. I cannot trust you to be a good husband, so let's just enjoy each other's company."

"Eloise, how did I ever live without you?" Richard said.

"Oh dear, why is life so complicated?" Eloise said. "No matter how many times we ask ourselves that question, there is only one answer: we are human beings. God created the world for us to enjoy—everything is here, and if we just stop to look around, we will find that life is great. We have to accept our similarities and our differences and thank God for being alive."

Although she teased Richard about having an affair, and she was tempted to do it, she didn't start an intimate relationship with him. He called her often, and at least she had a sexy, charming man she could talk to occasionally. Still, Eloise knew she didn't want to get involved with Richard; he was a narcissist and a scoundrel. John knew that Eloise and

Richard talked and that they had been lovers in the past, but he was not worried about them being friends again.

Human beings annoyed John; he was much more interested in books. Whenever a person tried to talk to him, the conversation went nowhere. When he went to a party with his family, he might drink wine or whiskey, even though Mormons are not supposed to drink. He did it to show off his independence. Then he would just sit and watch people instead of engaging with them. He felt like no one was as smart as he was, and he didn't want to bother trying to have a conversation. He didn't even like to go out to the movies because people exasperated him.

Finally the day came when Eloise decided she would walk out of the marriage. It had been a sad, lonely life for Eloise. She was the one holding the marriage together, just trying to keep up appearances and be a rock for her beloved Christine. Now, Christine would be out of college and on her own soon. Eloise knew that her family would not support her in divorcing her husband. Catholics don't allow divorce, and John was an honest man, a good provider, and a good father. Everyone would say she had to swallow the rest.

Many married couples stayed together without love and affection. Eloise didn't have any close friends anymore. Her only love was her sweet Christine.

Over time, Eloise had developed great inner strength. Her father was now gone. Both her godmother and godfather were gone. Her mother had developed Alzheimer's, which was devastating for the entire family. Eloise always prayed, asking God for the strength to carry on. Asking God to make her precious daughter a happy person, in spite of the environment she lived in. Eloise had enough love to protect her daughter and shelter her from everything. Her prayers surrounded her with goodness. Eloise often had dreams of all the wonderful people who had been a part of her life but were now gone.

Eloise and Christine went on a cruise to the Caribbean together, just the two of them. It was delightful, and they got incredible suntans. Before returning to California, they stopped in Florida for another two weeks. Eloise had some relatives who lived there, and she was tempted to look for property. She was totally in love with Florida; it was like Rio without Rio's problems. She made friends with a realtor and his wife, and they asked her to return to Florida with more time to look at houses. She decided to come back to find a vacation home—a temporary escape—and maybe one day she would move there full-time. The first location she looked at was Palm Beach. She would buy the property using an inheritance from her parents, and it would be in her name only. She found a beautiful house in a gated community with all the amenities. It was still under construction, so she could design it exactly how she liked it—five bedrooms, four bathrooms, marble throughout, a huge backyard, including a unique swimming pool and tropical fruit trees. Eloise felt great about owning her own property. The construction would take time, so Eloise would return in a year.

Back at home, Christine was doing well in school and was getting ready to go to a four-year college. Eloise was excited about her dream home, but she wasn't ready to make the move yet. She leased the house for two years to give Christine time to finish college. Christine was going through transitions with friends at school, boyfriends, and most importantly trying to decide which college to go to. She wanted to remain close to home. She and Eloise were very close, and she didn't want to be away from her mom.

Eloise and John had become more and more distant. It was like they were from different planets. John would spend every Sunday visiting his mother, who didn't like Eloise. What was sad for Eloise was that Christine was also ostracized by her own grandmother.

Eloise started to go on trips with Christine to spend some time away from John. Christine enjoyed traveling with her mom; they always had a great time together. As Eloise looked back at her life, she saw that in many ways it had been a good life. She never forgot to thank God for all that life gave her; she very seldom complained, and if she did, it was to herself. She had learned to be good to herself, take care of number one, always, because if she did, her family members and loved ones didn't have to. She passed this advice to her daughter. It seemed selfish to concentrate on herself, but it was her way. Every time someone asked her how she was doing, her response was always the same: "I am great, and how you doing?" It didn't matter if her world was falling apart; Eloise believed positive thinking brought positive results. She had the opportunity to meet great people, famous movie stars, princes and princesses, and she knew how to behave in the company of royalty. She had learned to be sophisticated and elegant without being arrogant or a snob.

As Eloise considered divorce, she thought about Richard again and whether it would make sense to get back together with him. Perhaps her attraction to him lay only in the fact that he was forbidden fruit. Still, it was tempting, especially now she was so lonely. John was a nice guy who should have married someone else—certainly not a Catholic from Brazil. Eloise started to hate the idea of being social and pretending that her marriage was good. She would confide in her family that it was on the rocks, and sometimes she would joke with her closest sister that it had actually fallen off the rocks.

Richard invited her to go away on a romantic weekend with him in wine country. She accepted his invitation. They spent three blissful days together going to a spa, wine tasting, taking a hot-air balloon ride, and going out to dinner on a moving train. They behaved like honeymooners, and she came back home feeling like a new woman. She needed Richard around, and she succumbed to the idea of keeping him as her lover. They embraced the blessing of knowing each other and being able to spend as much time together as they wanted. "What if John saw us together?" Eloise asked Richard.

"I don't give a damn. I have always loved you, and I was a fool not to recognize that sooner. What would you say to him?"

"Ditto," Eloise said. "If there are two people in this world who belong together, it's us, darling." And so it was. Time had taken them away from each other, but they enjoyed being together now.

Christine was doing very well in college and would graduate in another year. She decided to go on to study business, design, and fashion. Christine took after her mother in that she was poised and graceful and the main attraction everywhere she went. She had already been offered a job at two major fashion design firms. She could choose to remain in California or go to New York. Eloise was relieved to know that her baby girl would do just fine. Christine had a boyfriend whom Eloise did not approve of, though. He was a college dropout. His family was wealthy, and he seemed to be a spoiled rich boy. He was very handsome and four years older than Christine.

Although Eloise didn't think he was right for Christine, she didn't feel like she should interfere. Her daughter was over eighteen now, and eventually she would realize that her boyfriend was a narcissist and a playboy.

Once Christine finished college, Eloise was ready to go to Florida to enjoy the beautiful surroundings and her new home. She and John were living separately, but neither one of them had brought up divorce yet. Christine decided to stay in California but visited Eloise often. She had broken up with the playboy long ago and was seeing someone else now.

Richard came to see Eloise in Florida. While he was there, they took a few days to travel to the Caribbean. They were far away from everyone they knew and could be completely free together. "Eloise," Richard said, "unknowingly, I have been searching for you for years. The empty space in my heart could not be filled by any other woman, and without you, my life is empty." When Eloise heard this, she realized Richard had changed. He wasn't the womanizer he once was. He wanted Eloise and only Eloise.

"Oh, Richard," she said, "I love you, and I want to be with you."

"Eloise, marry me," Richard said.

"I'm still married to John," Eloise said.

"So get divorced," Richard said. "You don't love him, and you never have." Eloise knew Richard was right. It was time to end her marriage to John.

When she returned home, she told Christine about her relationship with Richard. Eloise was surprised by Christine's response. "Oh, Mom," she cried. "This is great news. Finally you and Richard are together." Eloise hadn't realized that Christine already suspected that they were in love. Christine became emotional and cried, but she was happy for her mother. "What about Dad?" she asked. "How does he feel?"

"Darling, all I care about is you," Eloise said. "If you approve, that's all that matters. Richard and I are totally committed to each other, and we are going to get married as soon as our divorce is final."

Christine had some news of her own. Her boyfriend had asked her to marry him. "Mom, I followed your advice," she said. "I found someone who is loving and caring. We are in love, and we want to start a family and make our home in California." At long last, life looked brighter for Eloise and her daughter. Eloise was going to spend her golden years being appreciated and cared for by a man she loved. As it turned out, John didn't even care when Eloise said she was filing for divorce. He was the strangest person Eloise had ever met, but out of respect for him as the father of her daughter, they would remain in touch.

Christine was soon married and pregnant with twins, a boy and a girl. Eloise cried so many happy tears and thanked God for looking after her beloved daughter. Richard and Eloise were going to find a place were they could be near the ones they loved—their children and grandchildren.

Christine's twins were premature at birth, but they were healthy. They developed well and grew to be the beautiful angels of Eloise's heart. She loved and adored them both. Christine felt so lucky to suddenly have two babies. Eloise was now a *vovo*, Portuguese for grandmother. Life was good for Eloise and Christine, and they bonded now more than ever.

Eloise, who was once also a tiny premature baby, had become an incredible person. She was everyone's hero and everyone's best friend, giving her love and support to anyone who needed it. She waited for years before finally making the decision to seek her own happiness at the side of the man she loved. She had to wait until the timing was right. Richard was married to someone else, and so was Eloise. They met again through a mutual friend and reignited their connection. Love stories like this one do happen. Eloise's message to everyone searching for love is this: don't give up. Age has nothing to do with it. Love is between two people who need and accept the love that God intended for us all. Search and you will find.

When Eloise lost Roger, she never thought about finding someone else to fill his shoes—to her, he was perfect. All Eloise wanted was to find someone who would fill the space in her heart that had been left behind when he died. Roger used to tell her, "We are strong. God made us strong enough to survive adversity and loss." Eloise never lost her faith in God. Roger had left behind the strength in Eloise's heart. Eloise was now passing the wonderful legacy of love and faith on to her daughter, Christine.

What is life without love? It is an empty space. God made humans to be with one another. He created us so we can love one another. Let's not make war; let's make love. From Eloise to all the people in the world: love is all that we have, and it is all that we will take from this world. Every minute, every second of our lives, let us think about what God gave us. Let us look at the beauty of our world and ourselves.

Eloise and Richard love classic love songs. There is one in particular that is their favorite song, "A Man and a Woman." Life is beautiful. Take a moment and listen to the music in your own heart. Love is forever. No matter what we do, it will always be there.

A NOTE FROM THE AUTHOR

This story is about Eloise, a character I imagined to be the perfect little girl who brought so much joy to everyone. It is a fictional story; therefore, if you recognize yourself in any of the characters, it is merely a coincidence. Read, enjoy, and remember that the message here is love, just love.

Be happy, improve your attitude, let go of negative thoughts, and live life today. Have faith in God, if you believe in God, and if you don't, just try to be happy and free. Yesterday is history, tomorrow a mystery, and today is the present. Each moment, each breath we take, is today's gift.

Love conquers all.

With love,
Alina Gomes

Printed in the United States
By Bookmasters